Praise for

THE INTERROGATIVE MOOD

"A fearless meditation on the sublime and the trivial, a hydra-headed reflection of life as it is experienced and of thought as it is felt. . . . *The Interrogative Mood* demands to be read deliberately, for it is courageous and entertaining and interested in the essential mysteries of self and society."
—*New York Times Book Review*

"Wildly ridiculous and laugh-out-loud funny. . . . Open the book at any page and I dare you not to be intrigued."
—Lynn Neary, NPR

"Can you picture the rabble-rousing literary offspring of Flannery O'Connor and Donald Barthelme? Does the prospect of reading a lawlessly lyrical, comic novel composed entirely in the interrogative mood pique your curiosity?"
—*Vanity Fair*

"The cumulative effect is of a latter-day Scheherazade, desperately staving off the final answer."
—*New Yorker*

"The narrative bounces along with assured rhythm, an inspired sense of comedy, and a style that feels artful without ever becoming chilly. . . . Powell's questions and non sequiturs will have you looking at your own life with a renewed sense of observation—and a healthy appetite for the absurd."
—Michael Miller, *Time Out New York* (5 stars)

"Offhanded, witty, original, and an altogether unique book. . . . Powell is a member of the badass gang of Barry Hannah. *The Interrogative Mood*, serious and laughable, extends this legacy."

—Rick Moody, *Bookforum*

"*The Interrogative Mood* may be the first 9/11 novel—maybe the first great 9/11 novel—that really nails it: The narrator is a redneck Socrates who has been given the green light through the chain of command to abandon the questions and water board. But he has refused.

Instead, he will ask the questions and only the questions. It's the most honest thing to do at times of great, wholesale uncertainty."

—Jeff Parker, *The Rumpus*

"Hilarious and sad and political and personal and ridiculous and capable of making your imagination explode like a lizard in a microwave. . . . Now, this book might sound like a great parlor game for stoners—and it is—but it's so many other things, too: a refutation of the idea that a novel must be a narrative, a war on ambivalence, a celebration of reckless open-mindedness, a reminder that the simple joy of wonder can still light up your brain like a spaceship."   —Melissa Maerz, *City Pages*

"A supreme literary stunt: a short 'novel' composed only of questions, each of which seems to implicate the reader in a narrative conspiracy as serious and absurd as his or her own life. Ultimately, Powell's little book can be seen as a word machine designed to induce unprecedented states of interior monologue, or narrative drug."

—Jonathan Lethem, *The Millions*

"[Powell] has a rare ear for dialect and dialogue, a dedication to new ways of making words jump and dance and catch fire."

—*New York Times Magazine*

"It's the world's weirdest conversation starter . . . and every few pages you'll want to pause to pursue a path some question turned you onto. Is it exhausting? A little frustrating? But also a pleasure?"

—*Austin Chronicle*

"A curiously fun thing you could imagine Tom Waits singing over a jazzy, beatnik score."   —*New York Post*

"There is a fine absurdist streak that runs through the book that is in some ways similar to Samuel Beckett's *Waiting for Godot*."

—*Pittsburgh Tribune-Review*

"This is a mindblower yet much, much more than just literary experiment. Nor is it showing off—Powell is a wonderful writer, playing with words, ideas, reality, you name it. A sample can't do justice to his work—you have to just surrender to the flow from Word One."

—*San Diego Union-Tribune*

"It's funny and philosophical and not afraid to ask, 'If a gentle specimen of livestock passed you by en route to its slaughter, would you palm its rump?' A short book in which every sentence is a question, *The Interrogative Mood* is a kind of stylistic Hail Mary, reminiscent of David Markson or . . . well, nobody really, but with better rhythm and jokes where the Wittgenstein references would otherwise go. Not that it doesn't have those, too." —*Village Voice*

"A peculiar and mind-popping experience. . . . Most novels take us away from ourselves, into the lives and minds of other people. *The Interrogative Mood* goes boldly in the other direction."

—*St. Petersburg Times*

"Literary experimentation of the highest order. . . . Entertaining and inventive, leaving the reader engaged all the way through without losing any of its steam." —*Twin Cities Metro*

"A wondrous, hilarious book from a writer who has long been one of our more wondrous writers " —*Buffalo News*

"*The Interrogative Mood* will leave you humming for days."

—*Creative Loafing*

"This book will sear the unlucky volumes shelved on either side of it. How it doesn't, itself, combust in flames is a mystery to me. Padgett Powell has given us a wake-up call." —Jonathan Safran Foer

"If Duchamp or maybe Magritte wrote a novel (and maybe they did; did they?) it might look something like this remarkable little book of Padgett Powell's: immensely readable, ingenious, witty, and ultimately important-feeling in a way you can't quite describe but don't need to."   —Richard Ford

"A delightful stylistic flight, and as engrossing as staying up late at summer camp considering every goofy or brilliant question that comes into your head. Padgett Powell is one of the best writers in America, and one of the funniest, too."   —Ian Frazier

"Intimate and hilarious—the yearning is as powerful as all that is evoked and revealed in this precise and beautiful novel."

—Amy Hempel

"This book is many things—ingenious provocation, devious and deeply hilarious riff, perfect party game, not to mention the most entertaining personality test ever devised. But above all it is another brilliant work of fiction, in some ways Powell's best, by one of the few truly important American writers of our time."   —Sam Lipsyte

"*The Interrogative Mood* represents superior value in a crumbling economy. Its 176 pages do not tell a story—they tell thousands of stories, all of them starring you. Powell pokes and prods you, soothes and slaps you. By the end you will feel as rich as Haroun al-Rashid on the thousandth night."   —Luc Sante

"This is the most unusual text I've copyedited in a long time—and I enjoyed it very much! Questions kept taking me by surprise, leading to much chuckling or my shaking my head, saying 'What the heck!' I'll marking the publication date on my calendar, because I've thought of several friends who might be as intrigued by your unique book as I am, and I'll be buying a few copies to give as gifts. Thanks for the interesting read!"   —The Copyeditor to the Author

THE
INTERROGATIVE
MOOD

PADGETT POWELL

A NOVEL?

An *Imprint of* HarperCollins*Publishers*

A hardcover edition of this book was published in 2009 by Ecco, an imprint of HarperCollins Publishers.

FIRST ECCO PAPERBACK EDITION PUBLISHED 2010.

Designed by Suet Yee Chong

A portion of this book first appeared in slightly different form in
The Paris Review.

Library of Congress Cataloging-in-Publication Data
is available upon request.

ISBN: 978-0-06-185943-4 (pbk)

10 11 12 13 14   OV/RRD   10 9 8 7 6 5 4 3 2 1

For Elena

Do you take it I would astonish?
Does the daylight astonish? or the early redstart
twittering through the woods?
Do I astonish more than they?

—WALT WHITMAN, "SONG OF MYSELF"

THE
INTERROGATIVE
MOOD

ARE YOUR EMOTIONS PURE? Are your nerves adjustable? How do you stand in relation to the potato? Should it still be Constantinople? Does a nameless horse make you more nervous or less nervous than a named horse? In your view, do children smell good? If before you now, would you eat animal crackers? Could you lie down and take a rest on a sidewalk? Did you love your mother and father, and do Psalms do it for you? If you are relegated to last place in every category, are you bothered enough to struggle up? Does your doorbell ever ring? Is there sand in your craw? Could Mendeleyev place you correctly in a square on a chart of periodic identities, or would you resonate all over the board? How many push-ups can you do?

Are you inclined to favor the Windward Islands or the Leeward Islands? Does a man wearing hair tonic and chewing gum suggest criminality, or are you drawn to his happy-go-lucky charm? Are you familiar with the religious positions taken regarding the various hooves of animals? Under what circumstance, or set of circumstances, might you noodle for a catfish? Will you spend more money for better terry cloth? Is sugar your thing? If a gentle specimen of livestock passed you by en route to its slaughter, would you palm its rump? Are you disturbed by overtechnical shoes? Are you much taken by jewelry? Do you recall the passion you had as an undergraduate for philosophy? Do you have a headache?

Why won't the aliens step forth to help us? Did you know that Native American mothers suckled their children to age five, merely bending at the waist to feed them afield? Have you ever witnessed the playing of shuffleboard at a nudist colony? If tennis courts could be of but one surface, which surface should that be? In your economics, are you, generally, laissez-faire or socialist? If you could design the flag for a nation, what color or colors would predominate?

Should a tree be pruned? Are you perplexed by what to do with underwear whose elastic is spent but which is otherwise in good shape? Do you dance? Is having collected Coke bottles for deposit money part of the fond stuff of your childhood? Have you inadvertently hurt, or killed, animals? Would you eat carrion? When it comes to pillows, are you a down man or feather? Are you a man? Will you place two hundred dollars in the traditional red envelope and give it to me? Have you ever had to concern yourself with the imminence of freezing water pipes or deal with frozen water pipes? How is your health? If it might be fairly said that you have hopes and fears, would you say you have more hopes than fears, or more fears than hopes? Are all of your affairs in order? Would you have the slightest idea, if we somehow started over, how to reinvent the radio or even the telephone? Do you recall the particular manila rubber buttons in the garters that held up ladies' hose before the invention of pantyhose? Who would you say is the best quarterback of all time? Between an automobile mechanic and a psychologist, which is worth more to you per hour?

Are you happy? Are you given to wondering if others are happy? Do you know the distinctions, empirical or theoretical, between moss and lichen? Have you seen an animal lighter on its feet than the sporty red fox? Do you cut slack for the crime of passion as opposed to its premeditated cousin? Do you understand why the legal system would? Are you bothered by socks not matching up in subtler respects than color? Is it clear to you what I mean by that? Is it clear to you why I am asking you all these questions? Is, in general, would you say, much clear to you at all, or very little, or are you somewhere in between in the murky sea of prescience? Should I say murky sea of presence of mind? Should I go away? Leave you alone? Should I bother but myself with the interrogative mood?

CAN YOU RIDE A bicycle very well? Was learning to ride one for you as a child easy or not? Have you had the pleasure of teaching a child to ride a bicycle? Are your emotions rich and various and warm, or are they small and pinched and brittle and cheap and like spit? Do you trust even yourself? Isn't it—forgive me this pop locution—hard being you? If you could trade out and be, say, Godzilla, wouldn't you jump on it, dear? Couldn't you then forgo your bad haircuts and dour wardrobe and moping ways and begin to have some fun, as Godzilla? What might we have to give you to induce you to become Godzilla and leave us alone? Shall we await your answer?

Do you ever suffer that sinus condition that effects exactly the sound of a raccoon in your head? Are you as much fascinated as I by the science and indeed art of artillery? Are you as much put off as I by the phrase "science and art," and more put off by the phrase "science and indeed art"? Who is your favorite painter?

Is your appreciation of a good material thing—let us say that pearl-handled revolver there—influenced by having worked hard to get it, or are you as likely to value a good thing having come by it easily? Do you value coherence of argument? Do you favor a day of the week? Have I told you that I have taken refuge in and, verily, succor from the Shodlik Palace in Tashkent, Uzbekistan? How much weight should a child porter be required to carry? Do you ever wonder after the stories stolen in Mr. Hemingway's valise on the platform in Paris? That he had no copies, that he had so many bags he could not keep track of them—are not these facts but proof of a boor and a brute who deserved it? Do you know what I mean by "it"?

Do you wish, as we all do, that you had a sunnier

disposition? Would you like to learn to lift weights? Are you comforted by the assertion that there are yet people on Earth who know what they are doing? Or, like me, do you subscribe to the notion that people who knew what they were doing began to die off about 1945 and are now on the brink of extinction? That they have been replaced by fakes and poseurs? That in ten more years, when everyone rides a Segway talking on cell phones imbedded in their iTeeth, the clueless world will be painfully immanent? That a large number of the world's folk will be fervently annihilating themselves, if they have not already starved, and a small number of the world's folk will be excited by rapid online acquisition of an exorbitant T-shirt?

Have you used the Tibet Almond Stick from the Zenith Chemical Works in Chicago on fine furniture? Would a good paper airplane give you a soupçon of pleasure? Provided you were given assurances that you would not be harmed by the products of either, would you rather spend time with a terrorist or with a manufacturer of breakfast cereal? What in your view is the ideal complexion for a cow? Is there a natural law that draws a plastic bag to an infant similar to the law that draws a tornado to a mobile home? Do you understand exactly what is meant by *custard*? Would it be better if things were better, and worse if things were worse, or better if things were worse and worse if things were better?

Have you heard the expression "the ragman," and have you any idea what a ragman does, or did? Is it still the case that you can buy build-your-own electronics kits from people like Heathkit and Lafayette Radio and Knight-Kit? Is a body catching a body coming through the rye regarded a good thing or a bad thing? Is there a reason that chlorophyll is green as opposed to, say, red, or is this another alleged instance of Darwinian accident? If someone said that a certain kind of guitar playing—I'm thinking of Clapton in Cream here—has a tubular sound, would this mean anything to you? Do you know that there are fighting kites? Can you imagine the fortune to be made were someone to genetically engineer a perpetual kitten? Can you see yet (I hardly mean to single you out: we will all look horrible and we will all look like old women) how horrible you will look as a very old woman? Would you rather have, in principle, fifty one-pound bags or one fifty-pound bag? Is the universe supposed to be running out of steam, or somehow is it getting new steam, or is it just holding the steam it has?

If the observation were made to you that "Strangers become intimate, and as intimacy grows they lower their guards and less mind their manners until errors are made, which decreases intimacy until estrangement exceeds that which existed before the strangers ever met," would you be inclined to agree? Do you know that a Gaboon viper is stout enough to knock a cow down? Do you know what is meant by the term "blackwater river"? In what area does your want of learning concern or disappoint you most, botany or mathematics? If architecture is frozen music, do we not deserve the whole cookbook of such recipes? When you hear the expression "Those were the days," or any equivalent allusion to the good old days, are you inclined to dismiss the speaker as a sentimentalist or do you credit that there indeed were better days? Do Darwinian accidents account for dogs and cats, and not, say, monkeys and possums, becoming domesticated, or does it owe to another kind of force, perhaps spiritual? Do you wonder, when you wonder things like who first got the gumption to eat an oyster, who first got the idea to *weave*—was not a moment like that *really* cutting-edge, as opposed to all the foofoo nano-refinements of today, which amount to the playing of checkers with the microchip?

Have I forgotten the question that goes here? Was it "Is it raining?" Do you regard rain as an anesthetic? Does pain purify? Are your nerves steady like those of the velvet ant, buzzing steadily across the lowly dull ground in its jacket of carmine velour and black satin? Do you know how to safely determine if the velvet ant stings? Have you seen the wall-sized bronze periodic table of the elements monument to Mendeleyev in St. Petersburg? Do you know that there is trash beneath it? Have you ever had antivenin? Why is it *-venin* and not *-venom*?

Isn't wool a marvel? Does it seem to you that ferries are involved in a disproportionate number of accidents? Can you think of any amusing confusions of the word *contraption* for the word *contraction*? Are you a taker of vitamins? What about confusing *confusion* with *contusion*, or *hypnosis* with *anhydrous ammonia* or *electrolysis*? If the blue royalty gets the red carpet, does not the common man turn green with envy and the revolutionary black with rage? Do you know what the actual song of a nightingale sounds like? Is the nightingale a real bird, and is it native to our shores? Whose death, recent or not, do you most lament? Have you ever watched high-rise construction? Would you like to drink cool clear water from a fat red hose? Have you eaten hot gritty radishes fresh from the ground? Do you appreciate that an oyster has, among its other organs, a *heart*?

This business of the ears and nose allegedly continuing to grow throughout one's life—can that be part of a great and benevolent creator's design, part of a malevolent god's design, or is it another inscrutable facet of natural selection? Is survival enhanced by a man's looking more and more like an elephant as he nears his grave? What is your mother tongue? Do you like to party? Was there a period in your adolescence when you eschewed underwear? Do you eschew it now? Do you favor peanuts, cashews, or nuts more exotic? Will you have a pet before you die, if you do not have one now? Do you grasp Ohm's Law? Do you regard cherries a fruit or a natural candy? Is intelligibility a function of the intelligence of the speaker, the listener, or both? Is it overrated? Is the human individual more important than the individual ant, and if so by a factor, what would you say, of what?

Do you like to carpool? Have you ever seen a large woman boil sugar watching the candy thermometer closely? Wouldn't it be better to have lived in an era when we routinely wore "leggins"? Are boys meaner than girls, or vice versa? Isn't acrylic paint essentially plastic of some sort? In what ways do you discharge your civic duties? If you could assign colors to the days of the week, what color would you assign Tuesday? Is the blue jay justly maligned? Did ball sports originate as rock sports, or heads-of-animals sports, or what, do you think? Do you take your bacon crisp or limber? *Terrefly* or *terrederm*—is there a word in this vicinity I can't think of, or is there a word in this vicinity that needs to exist but doesn't? How did the Chihuahua's head and the apple get congruent like that? Did you see the pair of little blue pants by the road? Do you think you'd feel better had you a degree in some kind of engineering? What kind of engineering would that be?

Are you much on games of chance, or cards? Is there anything sadder than the demise of the elephant, among all the sad demise of the modern world? Are you comforted by good tile? Would you like to have a modern house on a golf course—kitchen island, breakfast counter—and live a golf lifestyle with golfing friends of like mind? Would your terrors pursue you into such a house and life? Do you like to pay bills? Do you still answer the phone? Are you fond of country wisdom such as "All the snow in the world won't change the color of the pine needles"? Is the having of pets salubrious? Were you a bird, would you like more to soar or flap? Can you shoot well? Have you ever had, or do you have now, a soldering kit? Do you have a grasp of pH?

Is there enough time left? Does it matter that I do not specify for what? Was there ever enough time? Was there once too much? Does the notion of "enough time" actually make any sense? Does it suggest we had things to do and could not do them for reasons other than that we were incompetents? Did we have things to do? Things better done than not? Thus, important things? Are there important things? Are we as a species rolling together the great dungball of the importantly done into itself and making thereby a better world for the dungball rollers to follow us?

Would you like to have been a conquistador—perhaps a benign one? Perhaps I mean not a conquistador but merely a world-class explorer and discoverer—would you like to have been one of those?

Or are you content to sit in a chair and fret small, or not fret at all? Is exploring not merely peripatetic dungball rolling up? What about inventing? What about doing anything at all—is it not just making the dungball larger? My question then is, Should we make the dungball larger? Haven't we made the dungball large enough? Did you know that last Wednesday we were to have begun observing the Tertiary Protocols? Are you much disturbed by not knowing what they are, and that our failure to observe them will equal our doom?

Is a man sensing his oncoming death more likely to rid himself of his worldly possessions or cling to them? Does a woman behave, or is a woman expected to behave, any differently from a man in this regard? Do you quite credit that there are *burrowing* owls? Would you like to be a harbormaster? Which venereal diseases have you had? In your view, is a gesture of charity genuine or is it a kind of deep moral tax write-off?

Do you enjoy, as much as I, packing a few effects into a sturdy cowhide suitcase and taking a simple trip? Are you as handsome as you would have it? Would you prefer that the myth of the water skier skiing into a ball of water moccasins not be a myth? Do you approve of the terrier mentality? Is the sky the limit? Will there be green thoughts in the future? Are you given comfort or made nervous by ball bearings? I have a question for you involving "the velvet raiment of kings"—can you tell me what the question is? Is it late in the day or early in the evening, or is it the top of the morning or the bottom of the night? Is it fair to ask? Are you with me here?

IF A TORNADO IS a torrent of wind, is a hurricane a horrent of wind? Wouldn't it be grand to wear a good wool jacket with brass snaps in chilly but not painfully cold weather? Have you ever had to be involved in arbitration? What about traction? Are you well disposed toward bats or are you given the willies? Is it true or is it received hogwash that a meat eater wants a target in his endeavors and a vegetarian eschews a target? Can you picture the excitement of the day that gunpowder was first induced to blow? For tablecloths, do you prefer an oilcloth or an absorbent fabric? On a high-art/low-art scale, where do you put Norman Rockwell?

Can you tell a heron from an egret at long range?

Is there a connection between *tensile strength* and *prehensile tail*? When did navies lose the term "armada"? Will you wear polyester clothes? Is a cupcake sufficient for you, or do you call for another? Are drunks in your view guilty of want of discipline or are they guiltless? What distance is required to stop a motor vehicle going 60 mph on dry pavement? I see "red feathers" and "mud-caked face" and possibly "red feathers on a mud-caked face" but I cannot formulate the question—can you help me with this one?

Have you ever heard The Blind Boys of Alabama? Are you a circusgoer? Do you like to lick stamps? Has there been an American coin as good in its design as the Indian Head penny—unless maybe it is the buffalo nickel, or maybe the Liberty dollar? Do you know what chenille is? Do you keep up with popular music? Do you polish your furniture a lot, a little, or never? Wouldn't you like to have a grape arbor with beehives under it? Should politicians lie? Should mothers and fathers? Should children? Should I? Should you?

Would it be feasible to go to India and not be heard from again? Did you hear about the local couple who drowned in Nova Scotia? Did you know that I knew the man, and that I once saw him wrestle an emu into the back of a truck by himself, and that I am therefore skeptical that he drowned in Nova Scotia or anywhere else?

If you had the chance, and there weren't the certain prospect of time in court or jail in these our litigious times, wouldn't you like to participate in a rumble? Do you recall precisely how Santa Claus came apart for you? Is belief in Santa Claus, or disbelief, a kind of primer for belief, or disbelief, in God? Do you wear red? Does the having on hand of "spare parts" give you comfort or make you apprehensive a little? Do you feel closer to lizards than to snakes? This contre-temps about children choking on small parts of toys— have children always choked on small parts of toys or have they only recently developed this predilection? Isn't some charity to be extended the telemarketer? Is *orotund* a word? Can the spirits be lifted as, say, a quantity of wet laundry might be lifted, or would they need to be atomized and transported discretely to a higher plane and there recondensed (I am trying to evoke the model of molecular transportation)? Have you seen the expression "Unleashed is unloved"? And "If you love something, set it free"? Do you know the sport of so-called Indian wrestling? Did you know that I would like to have an early-model Ford and live on a dirt road and almost never check my mailbox for there would be, in this simple life I don't have, almost never any mail in it? Would you like to have such a red-checkered-tablecloth life too?

Would a catastrophic global war be required to restore us to simple living? Do you recall my asking you if you approved of the terrier mentality? And, in certain other words, why dogs don't (as a rule) bite us but monkeys (as a rule) do? May I now ask you if you approve of terriers themselves? Did your mother teach you how to sew? How far out of your way—I mean: you'd go a long distance to an obscure shop and spend a lot of money for it; you'd spend not more than, say, $50 at a garage sale if you happened to see one; you'd accept it if someone brought it as a gift into your house and set it up completely, with little trees beside it and real smoke coming out of it—would you go to have a model railroad in your house? Do you like fire? If you were to hear the phrase "does harm" in isolation, what might first come to mind?

Do you like feathers? Have you stood on an atoll? Are you familiar with horse tack and rigging? Are you barnyard oriented or is the barnyard a sea of trouble for you? When you wear white, do you insist it be spotless? Wasn't the world better when the term "haberdasher" was current? For that matter, when butter churns were in use? How did we go so wrong? Wasn't there a day on earth when not every soul was possessed of his or her own petty political and personal-identity agenda? Do you still do candles for your birthday?

Did you not have an uncle who was an artillery engineer in a war? Are you interested in the nuances of grease? Are you for or against canals, in principle? Is it hard for you to credit that dinosaurs *flew*? Do you know the average career length of the top-flight runway model?

Were you a thumb sucker? Would you rather argue with people or not? Can you think of a musical instrument useful in murder other than piano wire? Have you studied the soft toes of geckos? Do you comprehend with complete certainty how bonds work? Would you sail an ocean on a small boat? Do people who purport to know what a fractal is have a leg up on those who confess they don't? If you came upon a party celebrating something or someone with a yellow sheet cake and white icing, would you partake happily? Do you remember the candies called jawbreakers and Fireballs? Do you have a cutting-edge TV? What dead person would you bring back to life? Do you favor protecting the little wilderness remaining, or do you concede that there is so little left it might as well be ceded to the tide? Would a small red balloon cheer you up? A dog?

Are you fond of facial astringent? Have you ever heard the term, either in the area of philosophy or sex, "eggism"? Among these types of fences—picket, chain-link, and hogwire—which do you find most attractive? Have you ever worn a feather boa? Would you prefer to listen to a trumpet or a saxophone, both played equally well? Do you keep a personal bird count? Do you count calories? Whatever is meant by it, would you say you pad the nest or do not pad the nest? Do you have any formal familiarity with the architecture of arches? Can the slaughter of its own people, either directly (e.g., Byzantine Nike revolt) or indirectly (e.g., American "conflicts"), be regarded a legitimate tool of government? After what age do you think children are ruined by socialization? Given the choice, will you buy bread in a wrapper or not in a wrapper? What to your ear is the best-sounding language? Does the question of where all the garbage goes and how can it not soon not be able to go there bother you? Should I have put that a little more clearly? Will you wear a hat today?

What do you think might happen if "one animal, one vote" were conceived in the animal kingdom? How is it that ancient civilizations become buried over time? Why is oil oily? If you were credited with making a trenchant, lugubrious argument, would you be upset? Do you think there is really that much danger in putting a bird feather in the mouth? Do you prefer calm weather to violent weather? Are you fond of any board games? Does the notion of heresy strike you as serious or laughable? If your neighbors were a brick mason, a cobbler, and a butcher, and you were on good terms with them, would you feel secure in the world and buoyant? Do you grasp the principles of the thermocouple?

If you had a child, would you read to her every night? Do you own good silver? Do you regard yourself a connoisseur of anything? What is the most you have ever donated to a charitable cause, and what was the cause? Have you chosen the way you'd like to die? What profession to your mind most represents grown men being boys? Can you distinguish species of duck by their flight profiles? Is a red-checked tablecloth an agreeable unironic symbol to you or one that invites your cynicism?

If I said to you, "The sky today is beautiful, the white clouds and gray clouds and the way they are arranged, and the tops of the pine trees with their green needles silky and not stirring at all, breathless, though it is better, and would be better, were they, the needles, whipping and lashing in the wind of the hurricane we had, and this halcyon sky makes me long for that troubled one, but still, look at it, it is beautiful even today"—how much of this would you listen to?

Would you trust a vegetarian veterinarian? With your own dog? I mean, I can see how you might take the tofu-eating neighbors' dog to a vegetarian veterinarian in a kind of what-they-sow-they-reap vengeance, but would you take your own dog to a vegetarian veterinarian? What if there you were asked to fill out a questionnaire that asked if the dog, and you, were vegetarian? At any point in your life do you anticipate having sex again? If I said to you, "I want to return to 1940 and have a big coupe with big running boards and drive it drunkenly and carefully along dirt roads never causing harm except for frightening chickens out of the road, and I want you standing out there on the running board saying Slow down, or Let me in, and laughing, but I don't stop, because of course you don't mean it, you think as I do that a big 1940s coupe and careful drunken driving and one party outside the car and one inside and both laughing and chickens spraying unhurt into the ditches is what life was then, is what life was before it became ruined by us and all our crap," and if I said to you, "I have an actual goddamned time machine, I am not kidding, we can get in the coupe inside thirty seconds if we take off our clothes and push the red button underneath that computer over there, come on, strip, get ready"—would you get ready to go with me, and go? Would you ask a lot of questions? Or would you just say, "Shut up and push the button"?

Will you believe me if I tell you that I am a little fragile, psychologically speaking, and that there is an eagle over the woods out my window, and every day that I see him gliding around, with his white head and his big white tail, even though I have come to appreciate that he is as much a bird of carrion as a buzzard, or more—will you believe me if I tell you that seeing him gives me a small but palpable lift, and not seeing him a small quickening of depression? Assuming you might have as a child, could you eat Chef Boyardee canned noodles today? Have you ever noticed that when the coffee purists insist that the coffee-brewing equipment be kept clean of even traces of built-up coffee oil because it makes the coffee bitter, they are not kidding?

Are you lazy? Would you rather deal with fire or flood? Are you familiar with the creeping displacement of the American anole by the Cuban brown anole? Do you remember redeemable trading stamps—S&H Green Stamps I believe a major one was called? How did those stamps come to die out? Do you use a business card? Are you a sweater person? Do you suppose it's the case that damming some rivers is not an ecological hazard but damming others is? Do you picture the days of the week on a calendar in your mind? Are you afraid of a lathe? If we were bombed back into the Stone Age, as whatshisname proposed in Vietnam, would you have any idea how to go about making electricity? Could you even start a fire? Do you have a lot of credit cards? Given a choice, would you wear purple and red or pink and black? Were you spanked as a child, and will you spank a child? What's just about the worst thing you ever heard of? What's just about the biggest thing that ever happened around you? What's your name? What are your intentions with respect to me?

IF YOU COULD HAVE feathers instead of hair, would you? Do you think shop courses in high school would have more takers were they not called "industrial arts"? Do the very terms "gingiva" and "dentin" not sound frightening? Do you think "sugar water for the overweight" a good modern-day American equivalent for Marx's "opiate of the masses"? Do you give greeting cards? Would you take a short-haired dog over a long-haired dog, or vice versa, or are you indifferent? Do you carry a big gob of keys or have you managed to pare down? What's the fastest you have ever gone in an automobile? If you learned that you would expire tomorrow at 5:00 P.M., what would you seek to do until then? How often do you sit in a good straight chair and do nothing else at all? Have you ever seen an indigo snake?

Do you regard living with routines as liberating or shackling? How much of a baseball game can you watch? Will you wear rain gear or do you prefer just getting wet? If your survival depended on it, do you think there are things you would not eat? What would these be? Do you sympathize with the outlaw? When you visit old folks' homes and are mistaken by the senile for their own relatives, what do you do? Does this make any sense to you: "Pets at home. Glory. Man is but the percolator of his own retardation"? Do you know what exactly is meant by the term "a professional person"? Would you prefer to work for this kind of person or for the other kind of person? Are we in accord that whatever kind of person that is, he or she would not be called an "unprofessional person"? Do you recall, and did you ever try to use, all-metal roller skates that strapped on over your shoes? Are you big on nutrition, or is it something that happens or doesn't? Have Schwinn bicycles disappeared yet?

Could you wear a red clown's nose all day without explaining it? Are you a physical coward? Are you bothered by your cowardice? What are the top three things in your life you wish you had not done, or done differently from the way you did them? How old is the oldest human body you have seen naked? Is there a difference between a bobcat and a lynx? Are you more troubled by a lie or by a theft, or are they the same thing metaphysically? Is *metaphysically* used correctly there? If you could have a famous writer, dead or alive, write an obituary for you and really puff you up to have been something you weren't, perhaps, or otherwise take liberties with your memory, what writer would you choose? Are you good at jacks? Does it matter to you if the jacks are fancy with the little balls on the ends of the spikes or are just straight plain spikes? Must the ball be red?

Have you read much philosophy? Do you wish you had comprehended that which you did not comprehend, in your philosophy reading? Do you wish you had comprehended that which you did not comprehend in all instances of your incomprehension in all areas and at all times of your life? Do you regard yourself a dangerous person? If not, under what circumstances might you have been, or might you yet be, a dangerous person? Are you made nervous by getting on buses whose routes you do not know? Will you get on a bus in a foreign country where you do not speak the language? If they came back in style and it was not a matter of kitsch, would you wear a fedora? Did anyone instruct you in the matter of shaking hands? Are you baffled that there are people who do not know about the importance of squeezing? In intercourse, do you prefer thrashing or more subtle motion? If your family had a cat, and the neighbor across the street had a cardinal in a cage, presumably because it could not live in the wild, and your family's cat tormented the cardinal to death by leaping at and striking the cage, would you feel bad about it all your life? Is feeling bad about something all one's life anything to particularly feel bad about? Are we redeemed by regret? Do you like going into very cold water? When was the last time you wielded a slingshot? Are you any good? Do you remember Buster Brown shoes? Are you afraid of geese with red carbuncular heads? Can you ski on water? On snow? Are you prepared for the end?

No? Will you wear fur?

ARE BLAND-FOOD EATERS to be trusted more or less than sophisticated eaters? Is it correct to suggest the eater of bland food is unsophisticated compared with the eater of spicy food? Are you aware that the European rock dove, commonly called a pigeon, represents one of the most successful global invasions in the history of animal adaptations? Do you think the incidence of human homosexuality is higher than 10 percent? Do you like to listen to weather broadcasts or do you just like to see, in uncoached anticipation, weather happen? Will you be saddened that your life has been minor if in fact it has been minor? Is there anything you might do today that would distinguish you from being just a vessel of consumption and pollution with a proper presence in the herd? Have you ever spent time in the house of a recently deceased old woman and seen her Siamese-cat needlepoints and her baking supplies and her shoes and her inspirational sayings on the wall? Do you realize that people move on steadily, even arguably bravely, unto the end, stunned and more stunned, and numbed and more numbed, by what has happened to them and not happened to them? Have you ever heard the saying, Life is a sandwich of activity between two periods of bed-wetting?

Are there times when you are not motivated to do anything at all? Are you fond of pinball? Is good amateur theater oxymoronic? Have you ever been eye to eye with an owl that did not fly away? Had you the opportunity, would you become a worm farmer? Why is so little heard now of Tallulah Bankhead? What do you think the chances are that a man encouraging five-year-olds to wear their birthday-party hats as codpieces instead of on their heads would be reported to authorities by parents picking up these children from the party? Are you familiar with cultures that build their houses and heat their houses with bricks of manure? Have you ever seen a village idiot run from a dog? If your mind were in the gutter, would you pick it up or leave it there? Have you ever thought you saw a doll move? Do you know that part of the field examination for head injury is called the doll's-eye test? Have you ever been injured badly enough that your clothes were cut off you with those offset blunt scissors? Why do you think the hole in 45 rpm records was so large and the hole in the much larger 33 rpm record was so small? Do you support any kind of restitution to American Indians? If you could emigrate to any country in the world and support yourself there, which country would it be? If family is coming over, is it in general a good thing or not a good thing?

Are sports for you something to do, to watch, or to ignore altogether? Are you aware that there is a fine durable black wirelike filament inside the large gray soft strands of what is mistakenly called Spanish moss, and that this fiber was the principal material in automobile and other upholstery into the 1940s and perhaps beyond, and that moss was harvested from trees by poor laborers with long poles with nails in the end of them? Is there a particular odor or situation guaranteed to nauseate you? Did you have a grandmother who called the culmination of nausea "upchucking"? Among your relatives, is there one who is regarded as preternaturally sweet and one who is regarded as unredeemably vicious? If you had the opportunity to have a two-headed pet, would you seize it? Will you wear pants with elastic waists? Do you have any experience with chemical indicators such as phenylthalein? If you see something on the horizon you cannot identify, do you wish to go see what it is or to stay right where you are? When was the last time you heard someone say, "Who licked the red off your candy?" Have you ever started a grass fire? Are you pro blue jay or anti blue jay? Are you familiar with the viscosities of the various common oils and greases? Have you ever used a torque wrench? Do you have any friends?

How much will you spend for a haircut? Do you recall the last time you wept? Is there merit in carpet or is it pretty much a bad idea all around in your view? Do you grasp epoxy? Do you understand exactly who profits, and how, from the use of credit cards? Will you answer your phone without knowing who is calling? Will you invest in a fast car because it is fast? Doesn't it seem as if the heyday of hemorrhoid-cream advertising is over? Do you prefer to watch a bad game show or a good documentary? Do you recall ever helping someone locate a lost puppy? Are you familiar with the phenomenon of children completely terrified by clowns? Faced with an inflatable mattress of large size, do you attempt to induce a partner to inflate it, look for a mechanical blower, or get right to huffing? Do you believe in justice? When, in geometry, it is said "Let X be a right angle," are you okay with that or have you a frisson of doubt regarding this having to be said, and then regarding the entire enterprise of geometry itself? For good furniture, what is your wood of choice? Can I sell you on walnut? For industrial hand cleaner, are you Gojo or Goop? Do you have the time?

Are you aware that a chicken egg on its long axis will allegedly bear the weight of a person and that there are persons who can attest to this? Have you ever seen a commercial 1:24 scale slot-car track? Should the imminent extinction of a plant or animal be fought against or should it be regarded as an evolutionary punch that must be rolled with? Do you trade in commercial greeting cards? Would you rather receive a very good pair of shoes or a very good suitcase? Maybe I have asked you this already, but are you much disturbed by the prospect of putting a bird feather in your mouth? Do you think there is a constant percentage of people who are clinically insane, or is this a figure that changes over time according to immediate local conditions and according to larger historical forces? Is it surprising to you that more people do not lose it, or are you surprised at how many have already lost it?

Do you regard yourself a responsible person or an irresponsible person, and would you elect to be the other if you could? Does life insurance strike you as practical or as absurd, if not dishonest? Do you know anyone on whom you can drop in unannounced and in whose kitchen you might then sit and talk pleasantly? Are you engaged in a fight against clutter? Do you have in your mind an ideal color scheme for the inside of a house and for the outside? Do you like a forest of pines or mixed hardwoods? Have you ever seen a large game animal up close in the wild? Do you have trouble throwing things away? If so, do you ever retrieve them after a period of anxiety over the throwing away? Is it then easier or more difficult than the first time to throw the thing away a second time? Do you have a limit for this kind of behavior? Would you, if you could, be an altogether different person than the one you are? Given this choice, do you think many people would elect for a change or would they hold the cards they were dealt, as it were? If you contracted a disease that ate away your eyelids, would you shoot yourself?

Could you live on a boat? If a person split his time between Memphis, Tennessee, and Memphis, Egypt, or claimed he did, do you think that existence would be thrilling or crummy? When you are in charge of satisfying children at Christmas, how serious are you about stuffing the stockings? If you were told to draw straws (short losing), and the straws were a green pine needle, a yellow pine needle, and a brown pine needle, which one would you draw? If I told you that I am made depressed by a completely still tree but that I am relatively cheered by a tree with a little wind in it whose leaves flutter or whose branches sway, even a little, would you think me strange? If you could choose between a long stay in the hospital not knowing if you would survive it and a long stay in jail knowing you would be released, which would you take? Do you belong to a health club? Have you ever baked cookies that tasted like fish? Do you get all the work done that you should in life? Is it important to you that it be done? Is your life and what you are doing with it important? What percentage of people would you say believe their lives important and what percentage admit they are not?

Are you familiar with Trafalgar Square? Do you have it straight whether one can or cannot smell ozone? Will you readily neuter an animal? Do you find teachers of math dangerously seductive? Does a package wrapped in red ribbon bode better than one in blue? Will you wear polyester? Is it time I go? Are we done here? Have you had as good a time as I? Will you sing with me now: Oh let us be heroes, let us have emotions pure or not pure, be men or not men, let us buzz and rumble the hill and dale of daily insignificance just as confidently, just as threateningly, just as humbly in its cute red velour as does the velvet ant?

IF YOU WERE PART of a couple living in a three-story wooden Victorian house with a bad paint job outside and a shabby interior, to the extent that some of your rooms were lit by bare lightbulbs on swinging cords effecting heavy glare on the beadboard walls, wouldn't you consider it an appropriate diversion for the two of you to play Norman Bates and his mother at least sometimes? Do you take pleasure in cleaning and repacking wheel bearings? Did you ever wear a pair of Corfam wingtips? Would you be apprehensive about riding and handling a camel vis-à-vis riding and handling a horse? Is a camel related to a horse, and these to an elephant, and some or all of them to a rabbit? Does this sound like a tasty breakfast to you now: Atomic Fireballs, Bar-B-Q Fritos, and Coke?

If I told you that the single most distinctive taste I ever experienced was hot radishes from the ground beside the Arlington River washed down with heavy sulfur water, would you think this but the bluster of childhood memory? If I said that not even in France forty years later could one taste anything so fine as the crisp heat of those radishes against the cool slake of that caustic funky water, would you think this but the cheer of adult memory? Have you ever seen bluster and cheer ride together this way, like Butch and Sundance? Did you know bluster and cheer are good friends?

Is it your impression that people who worked in animation in the 1930s did more drugs than people who work in it today? What is the ideal percentage of cocoa in chocolate for you? Would you like to have been at the Alamo? Pearl Harbor? Given a choice between going horseback riding or skydiving, which would you take? What frontier of science about which you are ignorant would you most like to be informed? Who in your opinion was the greatest conqueror, militarily speaking, in history? Have you any skills in the area of weaving or knitting? Are you fond of tents? Do you like to have a wad of cash or a credit card? Have you ever been the target of small arms fire? Do you have a favorite brand of dishwashing soap or will any brand do? Do you prefer your clothes loose or trim? Do you know any knots beyond the overhand? If you found one drumstick (the musical instrument, not the chicken leg) on the ground, would you keep it? Would you rather see a season of bullfighting or take a course in machining metal? Do you remember *The Edge of Night* and *As the World Turns*? If you were sitting (say with a fountain drink and a lightly toasted egg-salad sandwich) on a stool at the soda fountain of an old drugstore of the sort nearly extinct, and a robber came in armed and commenced holding the place up, and you had a nice safe handy shot at the back of his head with a convenient good and heavy blunt instrument, would you take it? Do you find the expense of alterations at an alteration shop prohibitive? What about repairs at a shoe shop? If two people would turn the rope for you nice and slow, or at whatever speed you instructed, how long do you think you could jump rope?

How often do you ask yourself, "What am I forgetting?" How often when you ask yourself what are you forgetting does it prove you are forgetting something? How often, when you ask yourself what are you forgetting, and it proves you are forgetting something, does asking the question prompt you to remember what you are forgetting?

Do you have relatives to whom you wish you were not related? Have you ever dug up anything valuable? Have I carried on before you yet about how I miss the days of home milk delivery and drinking milk from those scoured heavy-lipped cold bottles, and how this want puts me in an even further more laughable panting for when a man would have brought ice to your door in a wagon, carrying a giant diamond-colored block of it to you in a big scissorlike pair of iron tongs, and setting it in your box, or in your cellar, and shoveling sawdust on it if you used sawdust for your insulation, or covering it with your heavy wet canvas if you used that, tucking it in as if it were a very cold and very dear infant?

Do you believe that I can still have any interest in asking you questions? Do you believe it is correct to call the cry of crows "raucous"? Do you believe in lions and tigers and bears or do you believe in the lord Jesus? Have you heard the phrase "to drink the Kool-Aid"? Do you have a steady hand for bomb making? Have you ever carpeted a room with carpet samples? Would you call yourself a good file clerk with respect to your memory or a bad file clerk? What is your favorite cake? Would you prefer to have sexual relations with a tall blond German or a tall blond Swede? Do you enjoy assembling manufactured items that are sold unassembled? Have you ever set any part of yourself on fire? If civil war or an invasion or other circumstances somehow effected martial law and the need to take up arms and fight, and your father was put in local command by virtue of his having been a combat veteran, would you serve under him happily or with reservations or not at all? Do you think he would have difficulty sending you into the Valley of Death as it were? Can you see him wringing his hands over you or do you see him snapping out your orders and getting the job done? Are these questions meant to distinguish how he would treat you, a son or daughter, as opposed to how he would treat nonrelatives under his command? Why have I bogged down so in this area?

Do you know of a likely candidate to replace me as the asker of these questions? Could you rush him to the fore? Do you know the story of the dog fighter Maurice Carver getting an injection for his impotence from Indian Sonny, the shot given him through the side vent in his overalls in Maurice's big Cadillac right after they picked up Indian Sonny at the airport in San Antonio, and Maurice thinking he feels a stirring in his loins and saying, "Rush me home"? Have you decided yet what historical moment you would most like to have witnessed with your own eyes and ears? Do you periodically walk around and check to see that "the area is secure," or do you make fun of people who periodically check to see that the area is secure?

Should children be taught poker? Would you like

to have a small pistol in a good wooden box lined with red velvet? And maybe one big pearl beside the pistol, secure in a dimple of velvet? Would you need any more than a pistol and a pearl on red velvet to hold you content all night until you could go the following morning to a breakfast joint and eat large quantities of simple food and celebrate being just barely alive?

We all know that pine trees do not lose all their needles at one time, unless they are dying, but do we all know that pine trees lose more of their needles at certain times than at others—that is to say . . . oh let's forget this question and try another: would you say that American rock music and American cars have their classic periods in strange synchronization, and that the two hottest periods were around 1955 and 1969? Is it fair to say that there has not been a good American car since 1969 and that rock 'n' roll was petering out hard after that?

How can men at drafting tables in pocket protectors in Detroit and boys in jeans and long hair at synthesizers in Macon, Georgia, have been so in tune? Is there anything you can take for a persistent benign sore on your tongue, by which I mean I do not suspect this is herpes related or anything else more serious than a topical wound that just will not go away and is particularly irritated by sour foods like pineapple? If you had a loud 400 hp 1969 GTO with a Hurst three-speed on the floor and the Allman Brothers' "One Way Out" playing as loud inside the car, would you not be unstoppable not only in all the serious adolescent ways but even now in nearly all of the serious postadolescent pre-senile ways? Can you list the things you are afraid of, or is it easier to list the things you are not afraid of, or are you afraid of nothing, or are you essentially afraid of everything?

If you yourself are not a coward, do you look upon a coward with sympathy or with disgust? If you yourself are not a murderer, do you look upon a murderer with disgust or sympathy? Why have I altered the position of "sympathy and disgust" and "disgust and sympathy" so? Did you ever try to raise two flying squirrels by getting up every three hours and feeding them cow's milk and stimulating their genitals with a tissue to get them to pee as your mother instructed you and seeing them die three weeks later of fever and bloat and fecal poisoning because the cow's milk had so constipated them that they had not, in all that peeing, ever pooped? And did you wonder later how your mother would know to stimulate them to pee but not that cow's milk would cement them up like that? And do you wonder now if she did not instruct you to tickle them with that tissue so they would "tinkle"? Do you miss your mother, if she's dead? Do you want to spend time with her if she is not?

Do you think there can be finer arms on a man than on a brick mason? If you are feeling low, will going to the barbershop or to the hair salon pick you up? What is your favorite sport to watch? Do you know the difference on sight between a rimfire cartridge and a centerfire? What is your position on yard raking? If you will excuse me for having deliberately bluntly phrased a previous question, and if you will accept that I am here again phrasing it so that reasonable middle-ground possibilities in your answer are excluded, may I ask you again now if, in sexual intercourse, you prefer a thrashing style like the flight of a bat or a subtle style like a worm eating its way through dirt? Will you go out of your way to get a wooden pencil or a wooden baseball bat? Have you had any medical procedures that involve the insertion of fiber-optical or other tubing in you that allows inspection of your innards? How do you stand in relation to the kind of cute crockery piggy bank that had to be broken once it was filled in order for the child to get the money she had saved? Are you much disturbed by the possibility of someone other than the child doing the breaking? Are you much less disturbed by the child herself doing the breaking? Do you travel in better underwear than you wear on a daily basis? Are you less likely to pay for a manicure or a pedicure? With what frequency do you drink a commercial milk shake?

Do you miss Tab and do you fully understand its disappearance? If you could have a guaranteed steady supply of an expensive or illicit substance or other commodity much prized and hard to get, what would it be? Are you surprised at the low number of people crazy or the high number of people crazy? Do you know offhand whether a hippopotamus sweats? If offered a cherry or a strawberry, which do you take?

If you had enough money to live on, could you see retiring to a small village in France and never being heard of or from again, and not speaking French when there, mostly because you can't, but also because you have nothing to say and you'd have no one to say it to if you had something to say, and mostly just sleeping in your quaint medieval stone cottage? Could you make do with a little exercise once in a while and a piece of Beaufort of very high quality? And maybe a look-in on the pigs? What if the cartoonist R. Crumb were your neighbor? Would you sleep better, or worse, or the same knowing R. Crumb was your neighbor in the next quaint stone medieval cottage in the south of France? Would life go on, or would you have to move to another village, or would you have to abandon the idea of retiring to France altogether realizing R. Crumb had done it and that he was the tip of an iceberg going back through hundreds of persecuted sensitive American martyrs, from the Josephine Bakers and James Baldwins and Paul Robesons to the precious Fitzgeralds all the way up even to profane California cartoonists—wouldn't you just be so yanked out of the frame that you'd feel it would be better to move not to gentle France but to, say, Burma where like Jeffrey Dahmer in prison you could be killed almost instantly when you set foot there? Wouldn't it be better to have a Muslim in Burma put a cobra in your suitcase on day two than go through the long pleasant sunset desuetude of retiring silently in France? Would it, in fact, not be better were you to assassinate ten or so pleasant silent American retirees on your way out of sunny France en route to your rude and immediate fatal neurologic toxic death in Burma? Would there not be cause for wild cheer among a certain kind of depression-suffering person who reads the headline "Suspected Slayer of Cartoonist R. Crumb Victim of Cobra in Burma"? Would it be the worst thing said of you that your last act was expended on behalf of the depressed? Do you want something said of you, or nothing said of you, when you go?

Do you recall that the milk in bottles delivered unto the stoop that we miss so badly sometimes turned to a clabber so heavy and yellow and thick that it could not be forcefully shaken from the bottles? Was your looking into this clabber—as rococo as bread pudding, as weird as a preserved calf—not unlike looking into your own crystal ball?

Do you like bright steel with a sheen of oil on it? Do you have any of those old pot holders made of colorful woven cotton loops? Have you ever contributed to a children's hospital or to an orphanage? Do you prefer a claw or a rip hammer, and do you know your weight, or are you hammer dumb—that is, is one hammer the same as another? Can you form in your mind the image of the slenderest person you have ever seen? If you were offered for free a rustic, comfortable house on stilts in a vast swamp, would you move in happily, or with reservations, or not at all? If I say to you that in my view all people fall into two camps, those fundamentally afraid of things and those fundamentally not afraid of things, would you think me radically overstating or oversimplifying? What is the largest number of people with whom you will do something as a group? Are you much of a cook? Are you partial to goat's milk? If you could be in a civil war, would you prefer to be there as a native partisan or as a foreigner not targeted by either side and free to witness the mayhem?

Those stamps I have asked you about before, surely—were they not called "trading stamps," and was "green stamps" not just a local more or less trivial name because S&H stamps happened to be green? Did you have that kind too? Did they accumulate in drawers? Do you have any idea what S&H referred to? Do you want to be buried beside your parents? Do you use perfumed boutique candles or utilitarian hardware-store candles, or do you use the one for nonemergency candle recreation and the other for emergencies? Are you handy with a splitting maul? Do you favor acetone or nonacetone nail-polish remover? How often will you mop? If you were offered a lecture about Descartes or about Alexander the Great, which would you take?

Have you ever seen blue hills? Does the word *Sioux* do anything odd to you? Does good leather comfort you or are you indifferent to it or do you in fact find leather morally offensive? Would you like to live in a neighborhood where children would ask you out to play stickball with them? Do you know the function for a parabola? Do you own a soldering iron? If you found a healthy infant in a basket on your doorstep, or anywhere else, say in the bulrushes if I have the phrase right, and no one claimed him, do you think the law allows you to keep him, if you want him? Have you heard, and do you credit, the speculation that the impending wars will be over not oil but water and that they will dwarf the present wars? Do you realize that the reason diurnal animals except us are not crazy is that they drink water whenever possible all day and go to bed at dusk?

Have I told you I have a friend who wrote in a book "Indians loved crowbars" and "They ate fat young dogs"? May I ask you if you have a friend as clever as mine, and may I say that I hope you do, but that I know you do not? Have you ever heard of the sexual practice of setting a person's buttocks on fire and quickly spanking out the fire? Would setting a person's buttocks on fire and spanking out the fire constitute, in your view, a violation of antisodomy laws or otherwise be regarded an unnatural act? Do you think it might be sanctioned or proscribed in the Bible? Have you been able to read the entire Bible?

What are three basic things you need to be content in life? Would you rate yourself as more tired than you used to be or as a person who still has all the get-up-and-go that it takes? When offered meat or poultry with a stuffing or dressing, do you first taste the meat or the dressing? Do you favor a hemline above or below the knee? Has your position with respect to birders changed over the years or remained the same? If right now you were on your deathbed but not feeling too bad and could have some one thing brought to you, what would it be? Do you like flannel? Is there a location or locale on earth you consistently think of as preferable to the one you are usually in? If asked to draw a circle, will you freehand it or effect a compass with the tools at hand? When you trap a rat in a spring trap, do you feel triumphant or bad? Have you ever knelt down and said to the rat, aloud or not, "It was a mistake, I regret what I have done to you, I wish you could now go on about your business, it's just that your eating my shit was at the time pissing me off, but now I see that you just had to do it, and what really kills me is how clean and innocent you look"?

Have we gone on like this long enough?

DOES INTEGRITY LIE IN failure? Do you recall the last time that you really had fun? If I told you that if I had a wounded blue jay that was content to convalesce under my care in a nice cage with pine bark in the floor of it, and that caring for this bird, and this bird's tolerance of me as I did so, in his nice fragrant cage, was all I needed to be content, would you think me a little off? Would you likewise take a dim view—isn't that a nice conceit?—of me if I predict that were the bird to not convalesce to the point that it could be released, but instead were to live apparently happily in the cage until I found it one day on its side, departed, looking up sideways with that terrible glazed eye birds get, that I would be then more devastated than a child? If I told you that I intended to take this shovel, and this fresh bottle of whiskey, and go out and bury my blue jay and never be heard of again, and I invited you to come along, would you come?

Do you know anything at all about the circumstances by which Leon Trotsky, in exile in Mexico City, happened to be assassinated with an ice ax? Do you find any resemblance between the mouth of a bearded man and a vagina? If you find a resemblance, are you unsettled by it or excited by it or left neutral? Do you like to sharpen pencils? Have you ever seen a woman of a certain age change the pants of a woman twice a certain age? Is there one enterprise or course of action you wish you had undertaken as a younger person but that you feel is bootless to try to pursue now? Does your tolerance for people about you increase or decrease as you age? Have you ever bought and used a petroleum-based spot remover? Have you ever used a petroleum-based spot remover that someone else bought? Is a petroleum-based spot remover something you will use if you find it but which you will not yourself purchase? Is, in your opinion, the work of a mental asylum good or evil? If you were to crash fatally in a small plane, does it matter to you whether you shit your pants before the crash, or after? Do you recall when your last stuffed animal as a child was lost to you, or do you perchance still have one? To what degree are you aware on a daily basis of coming into contact with polyvinyl chloride (PVC)? Does fair weather or foul depress you more? Would you think this assertion true: the ratio of blue snakes to red snakes on earth mirrors exactly the ratio of blue food to red food? Have you known anyone who has drowned?

If integrity resides in failure, does the abnegation of integrity reside in success? If it is the case, and certainly it must be, that integrity does not *always* reside in failure, but only when the failure is not casual and not the fault of a want of industry or ambition, and so on, on the part of the failer, then of course it is the case that the abnegation of integrity does not always reside in success, but only when the success is some evil stripe of it that someone has figured out the world does not need more of but that was usually thought of as pretty hot when it got started, like say populating the earth and land development—early successes, as it were, that turn into wholesale fucking disasters . . . and is it clear to you that I cannot for the life of me think of what the proper opposite of "integrity" is, hence this fey "abnegation of integrity"? Can you think of what the opposite of integrity is? Have you ever witnessed the effect a child can have on a drunk adult if he, the child, repeatedly calls the drunk adult a "poo-poo train"? Would you think a child who calls drunk adults poo-poo trains more inclined to a life of criminality than a child who does not so taunt drunk adults? If you were to travel to the graves of all your known relatives, how many cemeteries would you need visit?

If you find a bat on the ground, will you give it succor? Is it fair to say that cathedrals tend to be gaudy and overdone, and mosques clean and spare? When you drink from a water hose, are you bothered by the slightly moldlike taste of the rubber some-times? Do you credit that pickled things and smoked things induce cancer? Do you know the history or pro-venance or origins of Raggedy Ann and Andy? If you could get a dog small enough to transport in your coat pocket, would you get one? What would be the most fun thing you could do, right now? If you could suc-cessfully rob a person of his ill-gotten wealth, would you? Have you ever had to dig a large ditch or a deep hole? If you were in a streaming crowd being pushed into what appears to be a bifurcated tunnel ahead, and over one entrance was the word HOPE and over the other NO HOPE, and you could just barely manage to maneuver yourself within the crush of the crowd into either entrance, and it looked like a preponderance of the crowd was entering Hope, which entrance would you take? If you had a dog small enough to be transported in the pocket of your coat, what would you name it? Do you think in terms of salvation or redemption? Do you appreciate the color changes of leaves in the fall or is that spectacle a tad too popularly sentimental for you? Have you ever been catheterized? Is there a set number of rings you like a phone to ring before you pick up? Does the noise made by corduroy pants irritate you? Do you eat flan? Would you rather see a bay at high tide or low tide? If you could be instantly fluent in a language you do not now speak, what language would it be? Can you change a tire by yourself? Have you ever petted a vole or a shrew? Do you partake of syrups?

Do you credit that a man seriously advanced "Cogito ergo sum" with a straight face? How many screwdrivers do you think is necessary for able-bodied normal household maintenance? If there were a service whereby everything in your apartment or house could be made to disappear (called House Fire without Fire), without any mess or hassle or delay, and you would receive, in compensation, partial value of the material that disappeared, what partial value would be necessary for you to contract with this service? If you were to be executed and, by standard practice in executions, were offered anything you wanted as a last meal, and instead of ordering lobster or an impossibly thick Porterhouse steak or some peculiar fond dish like fish sticks and packaged macaroni, you said, "I want boiled kittens and puppies, and I want them boiled alive, like crabs," do you think there would be amusement, and do you think they would comply? If you were to be executed and you ordered boiled kittens and puppies as your last meal and they were served you, would you eat the kittens and puppies? Do you think you would keep a stoic countenance throughout your execution or would you get bad cotton mouth and then get to trembling or puking or jabbering or sobbing or wetting yourself or anything else like that?

Why do you think red became the dominant color for children's wagons, to the extent that it is virtually eponymous, as in "little red wagon"? Would you be interested in a rough safari up the Amazon? Do you know the different kinds of courses in which brick and block can be laid? Are you made a little more confident about things when you hear or use the term "hex-head"? Do you not think the next big disorder after chronic dehydration will be chronic asphyxiation? If you have a dog and you lie down beside him, do you prefer that he slap the floor gently once or twice with his tail in acknowledgment of your joining him, or that he lick you in the face and shovel his head into your neck and drive you off the floor with his boundless enthusiasm for you?

What are the instances in your life when you have been seen naked that you did not wish to be seen naked? Do you understand exactly what malt is? Do you understand exactly what sorghum is? If you had to be struck by lightning or by a car, which would it be? Will you use the phrase "forever and a day," and will you deal with someone who uses it? Does the word *thumb* impress you as somehow having a power or meaning beyond what it denotatively should have—I guess I mean, does it spook you a little, or sound totemic or talismanic, or maybe pornographic?

DO YOU FIND THE phrase "the verdant selvage of Michigan" intriguing? Do you engage in any ritualistic behavior? Do you favor the toad over the frog? If someone asks you, "What on earth makes the least sense to you?" can you answer? Do you have a favorite dinosaur, and do you trust that the popular images of dinosaurs bear any resemblance to what they really looked like, and do you have any idea how dinosaur scientists think they know, from bones alone, what the damned things looked like?

Do you enjoy taking cabs? Do you employ a maid, and, if you do not, would you like to? Would you name a child Jason? Do you know that the action of thirst or hunger is called "the mechanism" and that the mechanism of a pistol is called "the action"? If you could wear a loud-color pair of pants today, what color would it be? What is the smallest fishing hook or lure you have ever used? Have you lost or gained hair as you age? What national cuisine strikes you as the best? When, for something like a Halloween carnival, you want to have blindfolded children think they are putting their hands in a bucket of eyeballs, what do you use for the eyeballs? Was there a particular James Bond woman that you wanted sexually more than others, or a particular James Bond? How many push-ups can you do?

Do you know what the longest military siege in history was? Do you know that in candy making, in the timed boiling of sugar, you must use a thermometer— that unlike in all other kinds of cooking I am aware of, like, say, deep frying, you cannot just eyeball the heat? Would you think peculiar a man who upon the demise of his last pet had it mounted and swore off any more live pets? If you could witness a whirling dervish performance or a full-blown municipal riot, which would you take? What if the famous line "I have always depended upon the kindness of strangers" had been "I have always depended upon the freshness of air"? Would you feel better if you could put on a pair of good handmade shoes and just walk around? Would you like to go to Pondicherry? If you could reverse or bend a moment of history into an outcome regarded as the opposite of what happened, or at least as substantially different, what moment would it be? When you make a grilled-cheese sandwich, assuming you butter the bread (and if you don't, just take a break here), can you detail the manner in which you butter the bread? Do you find "in a New York minute" or "in a heartbeat" more annoying? When was the last time you saw a peacock, and when was the last time you were completely not nervous? Do women sleeping in men's pajamas strike you as affected, practical, or sexually attractive? Do you like burlap? Do you know the provenance of the phrase "suck an egg," and do you know the import of the insult "go suck an egg"? What has been so far the best single day of your life?

Isn't "in tattered array" lovely? Is there a connection between *beholden* and *behemoth*? Would you say that in general your affairs are in arrears or in order? Is that the same as saying in the red or in the black? Have you ever chartered a plane or a boat? Do you use the term "wiggle room"? Do you think of an angel as something that could fit on the head of a pin? Do you have long-term friends whom you assume are friends for life who suddenly abandon you, as it were, or at any rate declare one way or another that it won't be "friends for life" after all? Do you struggle against this attrition or do you accept it as part of the wholesale attrition of aging? Do you have any of your school report cards or childhood athletic trophies? Is the bone around the eye socket called the occipital bone or occipital socket or something like that? Would you pick up a lamprey eel or a hellbender? If you could grow your own coffee, would you? Have you ever managed to pet a chicken? Does the wholesale attrition of aging become in effect your not caring about much, or conceivably anything, the way you once might have, and do you see yourself finally caring about nothing at all or do you see yourself taking a stand for a few things, as though you might be heading for your own private senile Alamo? Do you remember the custom automotive gas pedal that resembled a large bare chrome human foot? Were you ever whipped with a belt or a hairbrush? At what age would you say your character was set—that is, when do you think you were you? Out of all the times in your life you have wept, can you select a time that you most wish you had not wept? Are you as fond as I of cobalt glass?

May I ask you to picture a garter snake eating a Christmas ornament and dying from it as a preliminary to subsequent questions I may or may not ask? May I hasten to add that this image is not mine but that of a girl or woman of my acquaintance who wrote of it? Do you know the delicate powdery tinfoil used to wrap individual sticks of chewing gum—is it not the case that this foil is very slightly quilted? At what point in human life would you say the nostril transforms from a cute thing to a not cute thing? Have you noticed the penchant of some birds, notably in my experience shore birds, to stand on one leg with the other fully retracted so that you think for a bit you have a remarkable incidence of one-legged birds who have adapted very well to their deformity? Do you think it plausible that a girl twenty years his junior could seduce a man by telling him of a garter snake eating a Christmas ornament and dying from it?

Is the altering of the trajectory of bullets entering water related to the bending of light entering water? If you could live in a culture where rugs are still hung out and beaten, as opposed to a culture where they are not hung out and beaten, would you opt for the rug-beating culture? Do you ever devote yourself to making a cake and then sit down and eat it? Were the Sunbeam bread girl and the Coppertone girl related? I have asked you before if you have used a torque wrench but cannot remember your answer: if you have, did you find knowing the torque gratifying or did knowing it strike you as fussy and recherché? Do you take pleasure in drinking from an old-fashioned waxed-paper cup as opposed to a plastic cup? Will you nibble a little at a waxed-paper cup? Do you know any dogs that have a pet stuffed animal into their maturity? Would you rather see a show about a military campaign or about a ballet? Can you knit? After what age do you find pothead jazz enthusiasts tiresome or embarrassing?

DO YOU LIKE A smooth pond or a ripple upon a pond? If you were to participate in a spice war, what spice would you fight for? Of which lost or destroyed culture are you most fond? Does sadness or irony reside for you in the delicacy of a rodent's nest, and in the pink hairless babies? If I said to you "tree wound" and "blood type," would you think there was a connection? Do you like a loose or tight inseam in your pants? Have you ever kept up or do you now keep up with a comic strip? What is your longest stay in a hospital as an inpatient? Can you eat a green orange with the same pleasure as an orange orange? Are "wooly bully" and "wooly booger" related, and do you know what is denoted by either term? When you play chess, are you tempted to call the rook a castle? Would you rather read about a leveraged buyout or the firing of a football coach? Have you ever heard the malaprop "brain truss"? How many jokes can you tell?

Were you ever involved in a seduction of, or by, a babysitter? What color most flatters you? In your opinion, who makes the best optics in the world? Have you ever hiked a little nervously in grizzly country and been assured along the way by the mildest-mannered and theretofore most sensible woman in the company that there is nothing to worry about because she intends to strike any bears molesting the party with a hammer? Are you anywhere near as strongly drawn as am I to the notion of the rogue water moccasin without having any real idea what defines such a creature or his behavior? Have you ever given a child a pet? Do you know if the bark in the crotches of trees is specialized and called specifically crotch bark? What is the term opposite to "economic downturn"? How often would you say you burn food? What is the cruelest lie you were ever told? Have you ever heard a woman screaming on the street and looked for the source and not found it? That question I asked earlier about the tinfoil chewing-gum wrappers—are you aware that the edge of the wrapper is pinked, if I am using the term correctly?

Do you wish to be in a thunderstorm or not to be in a thunderstorm? Do you like sheet cake? Does any one holiday annoy you more than other holidays? Have you witnessed the actual moment of the death of anything or anyone? Are you comfortable in drawstring pants?

If someone approached you saying "Lead me to the music," how would you respond? Is there a name to complete this progression: Rasputin, Robespierre, Robbe-Grillet, Robert Goulet, and . . . ? If you could spend some time with a young Judy Garland or a young Lucille Ball, whom would you pick? If you had house painters drinking on the job, would you provide them booze? Is there anything or anyone that you'd say you are "enamored of"? If you could disappear from your native country and live comfortably in another, what country would you choose? What is your position on the recreational use of drugs, and, if you partake, do you have a favorite drug? Is to your mind the phrase "cruel and unusual punishment" in any way oxymoronic? Can you define "ayurvedic"? If you were in a metal-roofed bungalow in a tropical country during a seemingly endless monsoon rain and were told that you were under house arrest and not to leave the bungalow, which instruction you could barely make out under the deafening rain on the metal roof, what would be your first response? Will you buy expensive stationery or will pretty much any old paper do for your correspondence? Have you ever crossed a river sill? Do you know what is meant by halberd and halyard? Do you sleep in pajamas? Do you enjoy defecating? Is there hope for peace in the world, all over it and at one time?

Will you be traveling significantly this year? I believe I asked you this before, but let me again if I did, because it is important to me: can you picture those old metal roller skates that had a metal shell or clamp up front under which you slid your shoe and a leather ankle strap in the rear to secure your ankle, the chief feature of which skates was that they had no flexibility or suspension and the wheels gained no traction whatsoever if you were on a surface smooth enough to pretend to skate on in the first place, and which, the wheels, since that surface was generally concrete, gradually wore down to sandblasted-looking remnants of themselves and became even more useless and treacherous than they had been new, so that the net effect of skating on these things was akin to ice skating on concrete? Weren't those old metal roller skates great? Would the equivalent today to the old metal roller skate not involve some Kevlar/Teflon-ey wheels, a microchip gyroscope, a laser level, a GPS, a twenty-four-hour customer-service support hotline, a built-in cell phone with a speed dialer to call it, a liability waiver/rider to attach to one's homeowner's insurance policy, and a streaming video feed into the brain of the skater of an exciting virtual landscape to skate when the skater just preferred to put on the skates, or think about the skates, and stay on the couch?

What would you say is the essential business of living well? Do you know that Native American tepee rings—the rings of stones that held down the tepee fabric for a tight edge—are still in place all over the West? Is forging metal somewhat akin to kneading dough? Do you depend more heavily on air-conditioning than you think you should? If you could eat but one meat, what meat would it be? In Scrabble, do you consider yourself loose or strict when it comes to challenging competitors' words? Where on a ten-point scale, with ten being salacious and one disgusting, would you put pornography?

Do you tolerate speech impediments in newscasters? Are you made nervous or content or indifferent by a landscape of red clay? Do you sometimes mistake Germans for Scandinavians? On average, how many times a day do you talk on the phone? Do you know precisely what is meant by an A-line dress? Can you clog? Are you bothered by keys that apparently fit nothing, and will you save these just in case or throw them away? Do you recall what the deal was with Howdy Doody or, like me, do you merely retain the obscene freckles and have no clue what he was about? If you were offered the opportunity to live in a professionally rigged hammock in the canopy of a rain forest for a week, would you accept? Do you believe in ghosts, or want to believe in ghosts but really can't, or dismiss ghosts outright? Have you ever made star-shaped structures of Popsicle sticks under pressure that explode when you throw them? Is there a connection of any sort between life after death and the leavening of bread?

Can you read music? Would it be reasonable to ask someone if he or she has a favorite musical note? Would you like to visit a tar pit or peat bog, or would you rather eat cucumber sandwiches on a pleasant veranda with a civilized hostess in England? Will you wear a garment with a small tear in it? Do you cry at movies where you are intended to cry, or at other points in the drama, or not at all? What is the highest value of theft you have ever committed? Can you recall the last thing you said to an acquaintance of yours now dead? Do you wear a helmet when bicycling? In socks, what kind of material do you like? Given its shape and whatnot, does the name Hershey's Kiss make sense to you? Can you train a dog? Right now, what is the thing or situation in your life that most confuses or baffles or paralyzes you? Are you satisfied with your intellect? With your body?

Is it correct to say that an orange is eponymous? Why is a banana yellow and not banana? When do you think the term "britches" lost its neutrality, if it ever had it? Have you ever been accused of, or accused anyone else of, cruisin' for a bruisin'? Can you recite the favorable economic arguments for deficit spending? Does pubic hair differ materially from nonpubic hair, do you know what the proper term for nonpubic hair might be, and do you know precisely how one is distinguished from the other? Do broken bones knit back together by essentially the same mechanism as a limb grafts to a tree? Have you ever seen any kind of live sex show? Are you comfortable around people who wear wooden shoes? Do you think dams have done great ecological harm? Does bodice ripping follow naturally upon green gowning, or is it a disconnected and more malevolent enterprise? Do you have any experience in the desert? Have you ever made an animation of any sort, even if just flip cards? In what endeavors would you say you have talent, and in what endeavors would you say you have no talent? If you could select an endeavor in which you have no talent and instead be magically and hugely talented in that endeavor, what would it be?

If you had a friend who, while watching a movie of the legendary porn star John Holmes, got incensed and said, "Look at that son of a bitch! That thing does not even get hard! Look how it bows out like that! That *son of a bitch!*" would you be in sympathy with this outrage or laugh at your friend? How often do you think about the mythic water skier who skis into the ball of water moccasins? Would skiing into a ball of water moccasins constitute an urban legend even if the legend predates the term "urban legend," and are urban legends inclusive of legends that are, like skiing into a ball of water moccasins, distinctly not urban? Does the *urban* in urban legend mean the legend is born among urbanites as opposed to its happening specifically in a city? Have you ever heard of the water skier who skis into a great ball of barbed wire? How would you assume these legends related: is the barbed wire a distortion of the water moccasins, the moccasins a distortion of the barbed wire, or were these legends born independently? Do you believe it could be the case that a water skier has in fact skied into a ball of water moccasins, and that another has in fact skied into a great tangle of barbed wire? Do you favor a lot of butterfat in ice cream or a little?

Is there anything you'd like to ask me? Are you curious to know what I'll do with the answers you've given me? Do you think I can make some kind of meaningful "profile" of you? Could you, or someone, do you think, make such a profile of me from the questions I have asked you? If we had these profiles, could we not relax and let them do the work of living for us and take our true selves on a long vacation? Isn't it the case that certain people are already on to this trick of posting their profiles on duty while simultaneously living private underground lives? Can you recognize these profile soldiers by a certain dismissive calm, a kind of gentle smile about them when others are getting petty? Is in fact the character of the profile-façade person not that which is called wise? And is the person who is congruent with his daily self and who has no remote self not regarded as shallow?

DO YOU HAVE THE locked and loaded feeling today, or the loose and dissolute? Would you molest a girl in a hospital room wearing a candy-striper outfit? Do you know precisely what a candy striper is or was? Have you ever seen a pot made of bark? What can you tell me about interstitial braces and dimensional stability?

Do you use the word *parameter* colloquially, and do you run with people who do? Do you understand the physics of the bullwhip? If someone proposed "alternatives to square dancing," what would you think he was talking about? Will you wear underwear previously worn by someone else? If you were faced with having a collection of bird nests or car fenders, which would you take? Have you ever heard the phrase, at least once used legally, "mental cruelty to a chicken"? Is life better or not better now that for the most part we live it without a daily concern with ramparts? Do you think that barbarism in the world continues apace but has shifted into subtler forms? Do you credit that there is a band called the Unhung Heroes with a hit song entitled "Look What I Found on the Ground to Mate With"? Have you handled fence staples? Do you know exactly when tinfoil stopped being tin, if it ever actually was tin? Have you ever with pleasure disassembled a perfectly good working piece of electronic gear and put it back together in a deliberately nonworking configuration? Do you like to have a wooden baseball bat around? Have you drunk wares produced from a still in the woods while standing near the still? If you have drunk from a still, was the still operator present or not? Do you like the notion of elasticity, with its princely resilience, or do you find something soft and undependable down in it? Is there anything in particular—above other things—that makes your day, or rues it?

Is there diabetes in your family? Are you scuba certified? How much will you pay to enter a strip club? If you got a puppy, do you think witnessing its puppy energy would give you yourself a little puppy energy again? Do you like to smell and feel—they'll squeak against your fingers—brand-new automobile tires? Have you ever paid to have something either sandblasted or gilded? Have I told you of the time my grandmother escaped the nursing home and I found her a block away on a door stoop expiring in the sun and she said to me, "What took you so long?"

Have you ever heard the phrase "to eat the either/or sandwich"? How about "chocolate and vanilla drawers"? Regulatory commission, tertiary syphilis, roundabout way of living, otiose goose, Bernard Paperhanger, pastel bloomers, doggone stubborn, stupendous city, beribboned frank, tallywhacker body, terrible, profound, large, stunted, and benign—do these things go together? How about gassated cheerleaders—the cheerleaders, say, had gassated themselves? I should say perhaps I'm a little unsteady here, but may I say instead I'm a little rocking horse here? Is the thing you notice about cheerleaders that while they do have those tight stomachs—I suppose by fashion one should say tight abs, they have no fat on their bellies—and it is arresting and interesting to see them, and this firmitude leads you right up to the breasts and your speculations thereupon, you notice how cheerleaders always seem to be refreshingly modest in that department, not amped out on silicone (I refer to the college girls, the professional sideline tramps are another matter), and you are on to the painful-looking perpetual smile that cheerleaders must maintain, and she is bouncing or otherwise celebrating the joyous routine, looking finally rather dumb, the whole thing rather dumb, not really her fault, or their fault, though you do fault her male consorts for being cheerleaders and not on the football team, what the fuck is the matter with them, and so there she is all hot and trim and bouncy and pert and full of vim vigor cheer and goodwill for your benefit, and you are supposed to want her a little and more than a little want your team to do well but you are nagged by this fact: you do not want her at all, and that not wanting has abrogated your wanting the team to do what she ostensibly wants you to want the team to do, and there you sit, a lost fan and a lost man? Do you see now what I mean when I say "gassated cheerleaders"? Can the feeling of not properly wanting a cheerleader be expanded, not unlike a gas as it were, to express your entire purchase in the world, your total stance on desire and life?

Would you like to have an executive maid who beyond a clean house would assure that you have crisp lettuce at all times and nothing gone bad and no bills not paid? Has it ever occurred to you that people could have—and once this occurs to you, you see that they *should* have, and you wonder how it is that they do *not* have—a batting average not for baseball but for life? Wouldn't it be handy to have a life average affixed to a person, so that a homeless person might be hitting .171, and Lance Armstrong might be hitting .338, Michelangelo maybe hit .401? If you had a life average, what do you think it would be?

Could you entertain the idea that what undoes couples over time is that they neglect to apply polish to the grain of their wood? Is a buzzard a higher-altitude operator than an eagle? Are you familiar with Chester Nimitz? Have you ever watched serious volleyball? Do you think the phrase "in conjunction with Uranus" is responsible for the accenting of Uranus being shifted to the first syllable? Were you to be in a fatal crash, would you prefer whether it was an automobile or plane crash? Would you wear a seersucker suit or dress, or do you now? Did you get Hegel? When you have captured grasshoppers—and if you have never captured grasshoppers, just take a break while I pursue this, it is important—did you notice when you sometimes might have inadvertently squeezed them a dark fluid forms a ball or bubble at their mouths, usually purple or roan? And was it your experience that a grasshopper so squeezed when released would retract this fluid to whence it came and be apparently no worse for the wear? Can you recall the reasons for which you were catching grasshoppers? Have you seen a bullfight? If you have attended a bullfight, can you say whether on balance you took pleasure in it or not? When you have seen bullfights—and again if you have not seen them, just relax here a bit, finish up what you were doing when the grasshopper stuff began if you took a break then—when the blood is coursing down the side of the bull in those pulsing sheets from the small wounds of the banderillas, and the big one from the lance, in those blinding silver waves when the sun reflects hard off the blood, and in those somber soaked oxblood-and-black hues when the sun is not direct on the bull's flank, did you think this horrible or beautiful?

If everybody is back now, may I ask if your predilection to order chocolate or vanilla over time has changed or have you remained more or less constant? Would you rather be in the hospital or in jail? Why do Americans use the article before hospital and not before jail? Would you rather be in hospital or in the jail? What is the best meal you have ever had (and forgive me if I have asked this before; if I have, do not feel compelled to give me the same answer)? If something could happen right now that is not likely to or impossible but that would really cheer you up if it did, just light you up like a child again, what would it be?

Do you know what is involved, with respect to leather, in tanning? Does a regulatory commission strike you in general as a good thing or a bad thing? In households in which a child has died, do you think what goes on at night in that household is radically different, superficially different, or no different from what goes on at night in households in which no child has died? If you were to be locked in a room naked for an unspecified length of time by a party you could not identify and for an infraction you could not determine, and you were offered a pair of wool socks or a pistol, which would you take? If it then developed that a big cat would share the room with you, would you prefer it be a lion or a tiger, given free choice? Would your choice be affected in any way were you assured both cats were friendly and that you had also, as part of the terms of your incarceration, to bathe the cat?

Was there an opportunity for you to have had your first sexual encounter before you actually had your first sexual encounter? Was it the case that you didn't realize it was an opportunity for your first sexual encounter? If you could, would you return to that opportunity and remove whatever prevented your realizing what an opportunity it was? Or, if you did at the time perceive that it was an opportunity, but there were other obstacles to the fulfillment of the encounter, would you have those obstacles removed and proceed with this first sexual encounter earlier than the first one you actually did experience? If there is a missed first sexual encounter in your past, do you recall the name of the person it might have involved? Would you be willing to share that name and the particulars with me?

Do you ever buy tea already brewed in bottles or jugs? Wouldn't it be sporty and fun to carry around a riding crop and whip things with it? Do you think of yourself as a quitter, and, if you do, was there a time you did not think you were a quitter? If there was a time you did not regard yourself a quitter, and you do now acknowledge that you are a quitter, was there one event or a series of events that persuaded you that you are actually now a quitter? In this context, or perhaps not in this context but in any pertinent context you

would like to supply, do you ever call yourself, specifi-
cally, "a pussy"? If you do call yourself a pussy some-
times, or all of the time, what I think is interesting
is that there must have been a time in your life, as in
everyone's life, that you did not call yourself a pussy,
either because you did not yet have cause to believe
you were a pussy or because the very notion of one's
being a pussy or not being a pussy had not yet entered
your consciousness—and what I want to know is ex-
actly when did this sound barrier of self-regard get
punctured or broken for you? Can you believe that I
once knew a girl a couple neighborhoods over who was
precociously blond and developed who had drawn the
attention of older boys and who succumbed to their
carnal wolving but who would apparently have noth-
ing to do with younger boys like me, and that brashly
as we hovered about her house while probably an older
boy was actually inside it with her or soon would be I
told another of the younger boys that it might be the
case that we could not have her but that I would have
her before he would have her, and that this boy some-
how relayed this utterance to the girl, who later con-
fronted me with it, without scoff, with in fact a note of
interest or invitation to stand and deliver, which note

I did not pursue, embarrassed to have had this brash-ness transported to her and certain that she found me inferior to an older boy . . . do you have time for this?

Do you ever burn loose threads back into place rather than snip them? Were you tormented as a child by perhaps a grandmother's saying to your mother that she thought you needed to have a "bm," by which she meant bowel movement? Have you seen a cormo-rant fly by your window in the early morning? Can you see me, when Jean Baker says "Jimbo said you said you'd fuck me before he would," say "Yeah, I did" and ride crisply away on my banana-seated stingray bike? Have you ever milked a cow or seen a milking machine attached to a cow or seen the udder washed with that iodiney solution called, I believe, Pro-teat, swabbed up under there sloppily with a rag while the cow stands there placidly, if not a hint impatient for the machine to be already on her? Can you credit that I never went back to Jean Baker's house again?

Did you try to learn to play the guitar as a child but fail to learn, and can you now not account for what happened to the pawn-shop guitar you tried to learn on, and are you a little mystified that it did not occur to you that perhaps you needed lessons instead of just diddling around with the thing without even a book? Is all of life clueless, or is most of it clueless with momentary bursts of clueness, or is it a spectrum of cluelessness to clueness on which people reside at various points, and are the points at which people reside on the spectrum of cluelessness fixed or variable? Would you expect if you have not been there that the town of Hershey, Pennsylvania, is predominately brown? What I meant was can you slide up and down the spectrum of cluelessness to clueness like a trombone or do you toot your one more or less dumb note all the livelong day? When people elect to not speak to you, should you not speak to them or deliberately continue to speak to them? If you elect to continue speaking to those not speaking to you, should the motivation be to pique them or to repair relations? If you could live on top of a mountain and grow coffee and not be rich but not have any real economic worries either and once or twice a day bury your face in a big basket of coffee beans to assay the quality of the product and otherwise eat good fruit and slowly read a book or two and wear good locally spun cotton clothes and enjoy seeing the weather come in over the mountains and sleep right there on the porch in a hammock and have a good number of dogs who maintain themselves without your having to mess with them and not be too bothered by your continuing to not speak Spanish very well, would you do it?

Are you familiar with a certain sort of hard-drinking woman who insists on driving nothing but the largest and heaviest car that can be had at the time? Have you seen a fox run gingerly by on its pencil-thin legs so elegantly that you love the fox and want him to stop so you could say something to him? Have you had very many forms of venereal disease? Do you know that the bark around the base of the limbs of a tree is substantially different from the bark on the trunk of the tree—one of its chief differences, if not the only difference, being that the base-of-limb bark will produce more of itself to cover the wound created should the limb break off or be sawn off at the trunk of the tree? Would the base-of-limb bark be called caudal bark?

Have you ever maintained a swimming pool? Have you ever been bitten by a rabbit? Have you ever studied the green shredded-wheat-like biscuits that come out of tortoises? Can you waltz? Is there in your opinion life after death? Is there death then before life? Wouldn't it be possible to get life and death mixed up and not be exactly clear what is what and when when? Will you use enamel paint even though latex is so much easier to handle? What is your favorite material in cookware? Would you rather deal with a man or a woman wearing overalls, and with which is it more disturbing to discover he or she is wearing nothing under them? If you could attend an execution, would you? If you could slate a class or sect of people because of its behavior alone for execution, who would it be?

ARE YOU GOING TO be happier in the future? Do you understand what is meant by cavitation? Are there dogs in your dreams? Do you have politochnaceous impulses? Do you have a polemical bone in your body? Can you tell which of the two preceding questions is fraudulent? Will you be exercising today? Can you recall the last time you saw, if you ever have seen, a woman in a girdle? Wouldn't you feel pretty smart if you were the one who worked out the equation for gravity? If a skirt were said to be hemmed with "tertiary hemlock balls," would you have a visual image of it? Do you know what mahjong is? Are you familiar with the apes that are very much like chimpanzees but either less or more violent, and are you sure there are not two such apes similar to chimpanzees, and if you are uncertain about any of this, does this particular uncertainty bother you more than other uncertainties you might possess?

Have you ever seen sparks issue from a wall socket? If you saw a large model train set and the engine issued smoke, would you say "That's cool" or just be silent about it? How many pairs of eyeglasses have you ruined in your life by sitting or rolling or lying on them? Have you ever seen a cork tree? If you were a creature who lives underground, would you prefer to be a creature who lives in a tree or would you hold your ground as it were? What do you make of the word *tinkle*?

Does any part of your character remind you of that of Fred Rogers, the children's TV-show host? Do you sometimes wish to sit quiet and alone and without a thing to do but sit there, or does this strike you as insupportably idle? Have you ever tried to pole-vault? What sort of height do you think you could achieve pole-vaulting? Can you walk on stilts? If you were offered the option of trying to walk around on those thirty-foot stilts you see in the circus in lieu of trying to pole-vault, which one would you prefer to try? What circumstances would be required before you would attempt to garrote someone with a piano wire? Have you ever eaten a candy flower of the sort used to decorate commercial cakes? Would you like to have a Lamborghini? Was your father a bastard outright, a medium bastard, or a light bastard? Was your mother a saint? Are you annoyed, or amused, by the playfulness of the preceding questions? Are you surprised at the absence of the whole-earth niche in the condom market—a biodegradable condom, say, or one made of organic materials, if not of something stone-ground then at least of something like Gore-Tex?

Is it legally possible nowadays to be burned up on a funeral pyre? Do you ever squeeze your own orange juice? Have you been in the presence of an accidental discharge of a firearm? Do you prefer diarrhea to constipation, or vice versa, if you have to suffer either affliction? How many generations back can you name your relatives? Do you remember seeing lion tamers wielding a whip and a chair—doesn't a *chair* seem an odd thing to have in a cage full of giant cats to begin with, let alone to use as a prop or standard instrument of defense? Have you ever heard it said of someone who drinks a lot but never gets drunk that he has a hollow leg? Would you like, right now, some pancakes with real maple syrup on them? Would you like to send a love letter to anyone? Have you ever mounted insects on a board with pins through their thoraxes? What aspect or adventure of your life strikes you now as having been the biggest waste of your time or energy or resources?

Would you rather receive as a gift a boomerang or a dead-bolt lock set? Have you ever in the first few minutes naked with a new sexual partner felt or thought you felt a vestigial tail? If you have felt a vestigial tail on a new sexual partner, or thought you felt a vestigial tail, was this an agreeable or a disagreeable moment? If you are asked to name the best rock 'n' roll band of all time, do you name it, say it depends, or say you don't know? If you were told you would spend the day in the field hoeing and were offered a short hoe or a long hoe, which would you take? Do you know the name of the condition that protrudes the eyeballs? Have you ever taken a girl to batting cages and there had her foul a ball into her own lip and had to buy her ice cream to stop her from crying? Have you ever lost a shoe and thrown away the second shoe and then found the first shoe? Have you ever known anyone proficient on a unicycle who struck you as a normal person—whose character, apart from the unicycling, did not strike you as deficient somehow or otherwise suspicious? Did you play marbles as a child? Is there a country or culture on earth that strikes you as better than all, or most, others? What to your mind is the most heinous crime? If you could, would you elect to have had more or better education than you received, and would you elect to have been brighter than you were?

Do you realize that when I asked you about what I called a "bifurcated tunnel," one side under the sign HOPE and the other NO HOPE, I was describing what I have since learned is called a gauntlet, this splitting of the route, but now that I think about it I see we do not really want either bifurcated tunnel or gauntlet because in my mind one is not yet in a tunnel that splits, one is merely approaching two tunnels so close together that they share a common entry wall, and what I want to know is this: if you found yourself on the left, which is where I envision the Hope tunnel, being swept by the heavy crowd into the Hope tunnel if you go with the flow, would you resist this default entry into Hope and maneuver over to the right to get into the No Hope tunnel, which you can see has a lot fewer people going into it, and which maneuver you think you can effect by some swim moves and other labors? If one of three planes was destined to crash, killing either the entire football team, the entire marching band, or the entire cheerleading squad, and you had to decide which plane crashed, which plane would you select? Are you very much into spelunking? What is meant by tartan?

Are you aware that there are accounts of dogs—rat terriers one might presume, or dogs that became the foundation for the breed—that have killed more than a thousand rats in a pit in an hour? Have you witnessed the sport called punkin chunkin? Do you know what is meant by defibrillation? Do you know if those large chrome-rimmed gill-like holes on the sides of I believe late-fifties Buicks were functional or merely stylistic? Did you scream when Vincent Price instructed you to in *The Tingler*? If you could have anyone on earth come over to your place for some sexual relations right now, or in an hour or two if you wanted to get ready, or even later tonight or tomorrow night or next week if you wanted major preparations, or, hell, like in six months or a year if you perhaps have some weight to lose, who would it be? Will you shoot a game animal and will you shoot a person? Are you weaker in trigonometry, algebra, or calculus? Are you a little bothered, as I am, that you don't know the classic patterns of plaid? Would you rather have written "What rough beast, its hour come round at last, / Slouches toward Bethlehem to be born?" or "It comes with the territory" or "Like, whatever"?

Have you ever been bitten by a cat? Do you know the mechanism of a calliope? Have you ever purchased a rubber from a machine, and do you know when that term ("rubber") disappeared, and if you could, would you replace the term "condom" with it? In swing dancing, there is two-step and three-step, but isn't there also one-step? Have you ever drunk from pastel-colored aluminum tumblers? Would you say that you are pro peanut brittle, anti peanut brittle, or would you say "I do not have a dog in the peanut-brittle fight"?

Would you not like to live for a while in an abandoned silver mine? Have you ever lied to a child, and, if you have, do you find you regret it more or less than lying to an adult? When your webbing goes out on your lawn chairs, do you get webbing kits and restore them or throw them away? Do you use bleach much? Would you say that in general Catholics seem to be intellectually superior to Protestants? Have you ever found live ammunition on the ground? Are girls in your opinion better looking in dresses or in pants? If asked to complete the sentence "Salvation lies in [blank]," how would you complete it? Have you ever heard of a bird bending a wire to use it as a tool? Do you know the current land-speed record? Do you know the word *transudate*? Have you ever been given help by an aunt or an uncle? Is it fairer to say that as a child you liked comic books or that you simply could not abide them? Do you know why people include "simply" in constructions such as in the previous question when very often the matter might not be simple at all but in fact complex? If you disliked comic books as a child, would you say the distaste was simple or complex? Do you suppose that a trained cormorant used in fishing must be acquired as a young bird, or will a captive adult, uncomfortable in captivity, nonetheless continue to get fish if thrown in the water on a rope? Do you like opera?

Do you know the names of shoe parts? Are there, would you say, particulars in generalities or generalities in particulars? Are you experienced in any types of eclipse—of the sun, of the moon, of your hopes, of a fool? Are you suspicious of folk who would use the term "barter"? Do you like caramel? What is the most agreeable and least agreeable barnyard animal for you? Do you understand the concept of tensile strength? Does shirking your responsibility matter more or less to you as you age? If you have never shirked your responsibility, would you say you are now more likely to or less likely to than you have been to this point? What if you had an affair with a homeless person you then dropped because you discovered the homelessness, overlooking the preposterousness of your not having known the person homeless to begin with, and then your friends, of whom you don't really have any but we'll say you do for the sake of argument, all dropped you because you had shunned the homeless? Do you like what's called Texas toast, and do you like calling it Texas toast? Have you ever thought you might be clinically mental to any degree? What is something blue? Are you fastidious about keeping the toilet clean? Do you know what an armbar is? Do you know anything about the Holocaust other than the enormity of it? Do you favor one kind of pear over another? Do you wear seat belts? Have you ever been to a VFW dance in a log cabin for couples only? Do you have in general a good feeling about a welding shop or a bad feeling? Have you ever seen straight pubic hair? Are you running out of steam?

HOW MUCH TIME HAVE you spent in a deer stand? Are you attracted to sausage (and to the *idea* of sausage), or are you repulsed by it, or are you sausage neutral? Will you get on a bus in a foreign city in which you do not speak the language? Do you wear slippers? A robe? Doesn't it seem as if fabric printed in a red-and-white checkerboard generally has squares larger than the squares in fabric printed in a blue-and-white checkerboard? Would you rather see Estelle Faulkner hit William Faulkner in the face with a croquet mallet as he reads *Time* magazine or the episode of *Amos 'n' Andy* in which one of them bites down on a roofing nail in a doughnut? Did you see the Tarzan movie in which natives bend two trees into an X and lash their enemies thereto and release the trees, tearing the enemies in half? Do you know your scat? Do you bowl? On a desert island, which strikes me as oxymoronic but the phrase enjoys, I believe, considerable currency, or maybe I confuse it with deserted island, which itself raises a question—namely, has the island once been populated and is only now that you are on it otherwise unpopulated—let us say then on an island all by your own self with nothing to read except one kind of poetry, would you select metaphysical, lyric, language, gift-card, or cowboy poetry?

Would you like to go on a safari, walking or riding elephants with a full bush camp carried along by porters and—does it ever occur to you that the good things in life have all been done already and all that is left is crappy new things or theatrical reenactments of the good old things? What about just wearing a blatantly stupid but somehow comforting or comfortable poplin bush jacket with epaulets in the privacy of your own home? Can you provide any help as I try to recall who it was and where I witnessed a man, I believe a somewhat socially out-of-it single man, in a suburban house, who was digging in his backyard a well by driving PVC pipe into the ground by hand? Have you ever heard of putting Mercurochrome on bait fish, as in "Put some macurreecomb on 'im"? If you own a crowbar, do you sometimes like to just pick it up and get the heft of it, admire the heavy hex shaft and the claw and the wedge? What color is your crowbar?

Do you bank in Switzerland or know anyone who does? Do you know anyone with a really good figure? Have you ever drunk mineral oil? Have you ever had a passion for airplanes? Would you be likely to use the phrase "inherent risk" or would just "risk" do for you? How many people have you known called Bobby? Have you played tiddledywinks? Do you like dogs? Can you sing? Are you smart? Do you like terror? Is fire a good thing or a bad thing? What upsets you most in life? Will you use the expression "Has the cat got your tongue?"

Do you prefer a red bean or a black bean? Have you seen porphyry, and do you know what is meant by porphyrogenitu? Is there an area of expertise which you developed when young that is incomplete but of which the limited parts you command you still command very well? Can you say why there are no longer TV shows featuring the loyal heroics of dogs and horses? When you see an abandoned toilet, do you have any impulse to salvage it or right it or in any way restore to it some lost dignity? When pelicans fly in a V, what do you think are the keys and rules for the spacing, and why do you think they use the formation? Do you like to visit grave sites? If we heard the ice-cream man right now dinging down the street and we scrambled for some change, maybe even from within the sofa, and went out there breathlessly and caught him, what would you order? Is there a particular Big Book you have on your list to read but just never seem to do it? Is there a similar Important Place you mean to go to? Does it seem to you that acne is not so wide a problem now as it was when you were growing up?

Have you ever rolled coins? Have you eaten a magnolia blossom? About that which cannot be known, is it better to be prudently agnostic or to go ahead and take a blind position and hold it dear? If you were to be executed by beheading or hanging, which would you prefer? If you were to design a wrapper for chocolate, would your wrapper be in general busy or plain, and dark or light? Do you have a supply, or even a stray piece, of surgical tubing? Do you admire the athleticism of jockeys? If there is life after death, would you think one should prepare in any way or does it conversely mean that no preparations whatsoever are in order? What is denoted or connoted by "tinsel town"? If you were availed a high-tech gas balloon and provided a little instruction and told you had clearance to take off, would you take off? Do you study your feces? Can you call to mind the single most remarkable or outrageous thing you have ever witnessed one person say to another? Wouldn't it have been more obvious, or natural, I suppose I must mean, that peppermint candy be green and white as opposed to red and white?

Do you know what an articulated joint is as distinct from an unarticulated joint? Have you ever had a meal at a soup kitchen or facility otherwise intended for the poor? What is the fastest you have ever traveled in an automobile? Who is your favorite western cowboy? When did you last see a pair of pinking shears, and did you enjoy the feel of their teeth on your hand? Have you ever played strip poker, and did anything good happen? If you were to be seriously looked at by the law as a suspect, and you were guilty, what level and what branch of law enforcement would you want doing the looking? Would your answer differ if you were innocent? Historically, what has been your flavor when you order a milk shake? Have you read the Russian biggies? Does any primitive people appeal to you more than others? What do you suppose is your upper limit, in terms of unbroken time aboard, on a sailing vessel? Are you enamored of Scottish bagpipes or do you find their sound unappealing? Do you know precisely what is meant by knurled wood? Of the children you may have known who were afraid of clowns, did they strike you then, or later, as well-adjusted children or disturbed? In your opinion, does the human brain receive a special benefit from chocolate? Can you number the kinds of private lessons, in all venues, you have taken in your life? If you were offered for free a genuine vintage carousel horse, with its steel pole, to be mounted prominently in your house, would you accept it? Do you know what green sputum as opposed to white sputum indicates? Do you dislike being late or not mind being late, and if you accept tardiness of yourself, do you accept it of others?

Do you know the location of Albemarle Sound? Is "Philosophy by Kant, Bag by Vuitton" funny? Have you ever registered a dog or other animal or otherwise dealt in animal registry? Are any of your teeth loose, or are perhaps all of them loose? Do you use the word *befitting*? I keep trying to formulate a correct question involving a man molesting a candy striper beside his hospital bed, some notion of its being acceptable to molest a girl under these and only these conditions, his possible dying or at least reasonable heightened awareness of mortality and her freshness in the red seersucker dress—can you help me with this question, help me see where we want to go with it? Would you think me peculiar if I said that if we ran down the ice-cream man and one of us ordered a Fudgsicle and the other a banana Popsicle, it would be perfect, a perfect order, and the only alternative would be if one of us ordered also a Nutty Buddy to be shared?

If you were given a fully restored cherry vintage automobile and a paid-for apartment in a foreign city and could have one other thing to go with these gifts, what would it be? Did your mother teach you anything in particular, and did your father? Do you know what "palisades" means exactly? Could you trap animals for fur? Do you have any gold coins? Are your knives sharp or dull? Do you trust or mistrust people who make a big deal about health? Would you wear chaps and nothing else underneath to a risqué costume party like Carnival? Do you have a favorite candy bar? Do you do a good job when you wash windows or does something always seem to be left undone, perhaps putting you in that inside-outside debate? If you had a little booklet of Post-its printed up to say "Repair in order," how many of these would you properly have to apply to things around your house or apartment or life in general?

Can you stand Pat Boone? Are you daft? Are you going to Funkytown? Can you excuse me for that impertinence? That is to say, can you simply without prejudice not answer the ante-penultimate question?

WOULD YOU LIKE TO live a life that allows for frequent use of acronym, as in "Let's proceed according to SOP?" Would you rather have a swimming pool or a small private gymnasium? Do you have any experience that suggests there was a higher water table when you were a child than there is now? Do you recall that once chinchilla farming was advertised in the back of a lot of magazines, with perhaps the same frequency and in the position that the Chia Pet was advertised later? Would you agree with me if I said that the shotgun, when configured for sport and not for bank robbing, etc., is a friendlier weapon than a rifle or a pistol? Has the importance of "being a gentleman," if not also what is meant by being a gentleman, and why one should be one, and who can or should be one, changed over time? Have you heard the expression "Pats on the back in high school become kicks in the ass in life"?

The terrible twining calipers lifted the boy's

brain from its pan—does this frighten you, amuse you, or leave you indifferent? Is it a sound observation that a bird soars in direct relation to its proclivity to eat carrion, and flies in direct relation to its proclivity to hunt live prey? If you were in a besieged medieval castle or garrison or town, can you imagine something worse than the enemy's lobbing over your walls a putrid cow that exploded on impact and got on you? I guess a load of flaming canisters that burned you or a thousand plague-carrying live rats lofted over and bursting from their confines might in the end exceed a cow in terms of projected damage, but doesn't that putrid cow somehow still take the cake? Are you very appreciative of Yeats? Are you more fond of maple syrup or honey? Do you go to church? Do you believe?

Do you enjoy taking narcotics? Have you ever had a biopsy performed on a sensitive area, such as the tongue? Does it bother you, or thrill you, to spend holidays intended for conviviality alone? How late in life do you think it is reasonable to anticipate the excitement of meeting a new lover? Would you like to live for a good period of time in India? What would you think an Uzi machine gun might cost? If you had to sleep overnight confined with a polar bear or an anaconda, which would you pick? If you could be reeducated from the ground up by world-class teachers in either literature or mathematics, which field would you take? Do you like shoes or are they just necessary baggage? Do you know anything about cement?

If a woman were to tell you "I'm a pretty darn good cook if I must say so myself" and then offer you meat loaf or spaghetti, which would you take? Would you prefer to go fishing beside the rich on a pristine mountain stream or beside the poor on a polluted canal? Have you ever spent time with European youth who regard themselves revolutionaries? Have you ever spent time with European youth who regard themselves revolutionaries who did not smoke? Did they not smoke to the extent that it wasn't the cloying annoying asphyxiating politics that got you, but the smoke? If you decide to have, and set out to execute, "a really good day" for yourself, does it work or often not work? Have you ever seen an unfriendly Dalmatian?

Would you rather be beaten with a board or a chain? Does any particular person strike you as the most intelligent you have seen or known? Have you ever participated in a cakewalk? What do you take on popcorn? Do you know what is meant by high explosive? What term would most accurately oppose the term "rigorous argument"? Would you rather spend an hour driving a hot rod or talking to a whore? If you could elect to find yourself in a mahogany Chris-Craft powerboat on Lake Michigan in 1930 and then live out the life of that person in that time without returning to your life in this time, would you? Have you ever bred mice? Do you like tar? Do you know much about plate tectonics? Do you regard yourself as redeemed, redeemable, or irretrievably lost? Do you find that the flavor butter pecan, as in butter-pecan ice cream, sounds better than it tastes? What is the loudest noise you have ever heard? Have you done any mountain climbing? Would you eat a monkey? What broke your heart?

When the going gets tough, are you one of the tough that gets going? Have you ever dreamed you had apartments you were only sometimes aware you had? Do you have any ballet training, and if not, would you like some? Have you ever seen Newton's *Optiks*? I have a vision of Debbie Marsden in a light blue dress saying somewhat proudly as we did the dishes that we would not do the flatware because "Mommie scalds these"; have you ever heard of someone boiling the silverware in her own household? Do you think Debbie Marsden might have become maladjusted somehow? Do you think there is any statistical merit to the possibility that quiet shy girls stand a chance higher in proportion to that of more robust girls of turning nymphomaniac?

What is it called when a color has a white chalkiness in it? Are you troubled by the fact that tweezers are generally so poorly made that they do not grip anything well? Are you comforted by having a good tool in your hand whether you are to do anything with it or not, or even if you do not know how to use the tool? If we were to scramble for change because we heard the ice-cream man coming, on our knees digging into the recesses of the sofa with the cushions on top of our arms, and we sensed the ice-cream man was passing by and we had found no change so we just relaxed there with our arms outstretched and our faces on the knobby sofa cushions, how long could we hold the position, what could we talk about, and do you think we could be relatively content there or would we be impatient to get up and brush ourselves off and put our adult selves back together and be on about the important business of our lives?

DO YOU TAKE PLEASURE in wiping a surface clean? If you lived in a little bunk on a big boat or barge and anything you had onboard had to be in the aggregate about the size of a toaster, what would you have onboard? Would you prefer for company a goat or a sheep? What kind of person have you heard use the term "upchuck"? When someone upchucks near you, do you ever also upchuck? When was the last time you went to church? Do you recall the last conversation you had with your parents? If you could choose between sanding something valuable until there was a good surface on it and then painting it correctly with a good paint or varnish and having it look wonderful, or setting something worthless on fire and having it burn until there was absolutely nothing left of it but a handsome pile of ash, which endeavor would you take?

What is the largest zone of neglect in your life? Do you enjoy the study of physics? Have your own forays into plumbing been successful? Do you wonder more what has become of the normal people you have known or the weird people you have known? If you were the victim of a violent crime or a close member of your family was the victim and the perp alleged a junk-food defense, would you be more upset or less upset than if he did not allege a junk-food defense? Do you have a shorter temper than usual with a person who is snapping chewing gum? For New Year's Eve, do you prefer a big loud drunk party at which say someone pogos nude across the room, or would you like to stand beside a tree alone and see if there is any wind in it?

What is your favorite fabric? Have you ever raised a wild baby bird? Which of your parents would you say was the more selfish? Do you have the patience for pickup sticks? Do you like high-tech gadgetry? Are there any significant personal betrayals in your past, to you or by you? Do you know what is meant exactly by synthetic motor oil? Do you know what famous person complained famously that many men produce only excrement? If a man completed building a model airplane and ordered a subscription to a newspaper on a given day, would he have been more productive than if he had only produced excrement? Would he be better than they if he wrote a beautiful piece of music that was listened to by hundreds of men or even thousands as they produced only excrement? What if a couple of them or even hundreds annoyed by the music turn it off as they produce only excrement? What if the excrement producers regard as holy more or less that production and admit no distraction from their mission? What if they yell from the chamber where they ply their industry "Turn that crap off!" speaking of the music that someone has thoughtlessly left playing at too high a volume for their comfort? What if they have one of those German shelf toilets that allows the inspection of the feces and as they inspect the feces it is established that no one is so inspecting the music to ascertain its quality? Things are a little different now that we have some quality control going down on the excrement end and no quality control going down on the productive-geniuses-live-better-lives end, aren't they?

Will you forgive me my impertinence? Would you be persuaded to do so by the news that perhaps I was overindulging my pain pills against the impending medical adjudication as to whether or not my recent biopsy is malignant? Do you traffic much in facial creams and lotions and such? Do you breathe correctly, as, say, you are wont to be taught in yoga environs, or do you just breathe any which old way?

When did you last have a piece of Melba toast? Are you familiar with the particular dead quality of the Suwannee River with respect to fish? Do you listen to the music of the spheres or do you dance a dull sublunary ditty?

What percentage of men or women have the capacity, or historically have had the capacity, to declare war? Do you keep a balanced checkbook? Would you take a red-colored dog or a white-colored dog? Do your shoes fit well? Do you know that in some countries men do all the public cooking and women do all the private cooking? Do you know that for some time I have wanted to ask you a question relating to bolos and boomerangs but that I cannot figure out the question? Do you know which is the stouter snake, Russell's or Gaboon's viper? Do you prefer a home brew for cleaning windows or a commercial formula like Windex? What is it called when a product begins to serve as the generic term for that class of things the product is a member of, as in Scotch tape, make a Xerox of that, get me a Kleenex, and so on? Would you include "Magic Marker" in this category of eponymous generics?

Have you seen a person recently so delicious-looking that, were you and this person to be scrambling for ice-cream change with your arms in the sofa and your faces laid on the cushions looking at each other as you felt for coins and the ice-cream truck dinged on by and your hands in there felt only the lint of the sofa scrofula and your faces were fairly close across a distance of that knobby nylon terrain, you might feel compelled to slide your face toward this delicious-looking person's and kiss him or her—have you seen anyone like this recently? Would you like to see a person so delicious-looking that you might feel compelled to try to kiss the person without, as it were, propriety? Do you know what conservative bone-fracture management might mean as opposed to nonconservative bone-fracture management? Would you take a ballet class now?

When you go to a football game, will you wave a towel for your team? Do you have any mounted animals or pelts? Do you ever have a notion such as "Today would be a good day for me to use a lever on something"? Are you very happy with your hands or could they be other hands and suit you better? Can you quickly name a good thing and a bad thing? Do you understand really how a radio works? Do you eat cake for the icing or icing for the cake? What is the best narcotic in your experience? Am I the only one who thinks CBS should be prosecuted for getting rid of Jill Arrington over the nipple erection during the Florida-Tennessee game? Of course they covered their tracks and will not be found accountable, but the fact remains that someone owes Jill an apology, don't you think? Would that apology of course not be tantamount to the entire United States' apologizing for its Puritan hysteria and hypocrisies—to apologizing for its very existence? Can someone explain successfully why commercials for erectile dysfunction are allowed to frame the verboten erect-nipple episode? Is it because the impotence-pill commercial is the revenue-generating vehicle that just happens to televise the nipple? Is the impotence-pill commercial a medical issue while the nipple is in obvious good health—that is, is nonworking sex okay but working sex not okay? Is there any end to the inane ways one can phrase this stupid question about a stupid country?

CAN YOU COOK? Can you fight? Can you lie? Can you do anything well? Have you acquired a sufficient stock of clothes from a mail-order seller that you can, if you want to, flip through the catalog to decide what to wear that day? Do you know a peony from a petunia? What exactly does "Standard & Poor" mean to you? Can you hang ten? Do you dance? Do you view extreme sports as legitimate enterprises or are they just imprudent fucking around until you get hurt? Can the same question not be asked of sexual consort? Has it been a while since you cracked a can of ready-made biscuits over the counter and felt that gratifying modest explosion of clammy dough in your hand?

Are you given to the canary or the parakeet? Does the prospect of a pet's outliving you give you pause? Can we relax and trust that our wishes in these regards, our posthumous affairs as it were, will really be administered as we have stipulated, or will we be frustrated and yelling through the glass walls of heaven or the hot opaque obsidian walls of hell at the corrupt disregard for our eternal wishes? What if you saw, from heaven, your macaw starve in its cage? What if you saw your horse led to the glue factory?

How many people per hundred would you say are asses? Should non-asses have to put up with asses? Should asses have to put up with non-asses? Who deserves less having to endure the other? Does it seem that by definition an ass is not so bothered by things as a non-ass? Is it fair to say, in fact, that asses are the unbothered and non-asses are the bothered? Do you think the bothered were really meant to inherit the earth?

Do you know that since I last asked you about the disappearance of the blue jay—I meant to, if I did not—that I have found one blue jay feather under my house? Would a complete familiarization with the military campaigns of Napoleon provide the modern-day general with much of value, or little of value, or a medium quantity of value in terms of what is called the necessary skill set for a general today? Are you innocent of *The Nutcracker* ballet or are you of the surprising number of people who see *The Nutcracker* ballet every year? If a dog needs to be shaved because it is overheating but the haircut embarrasses the dog, should it be shaved anyway? Do you sometimes ice a part of your body gratuitously? When was the last time you gapped a spark plug yourself? Would you rather be bitten by an alligator or a large cat? How many diapers would you say you have changed in your life?

"Why must it all suck so bad?"—is this a question asked by a suicide candidate or a comedian? Does turmeric lift the spirits or just dye everything? Do you loosen your pants after eating? Do you realize that on Sunday-morning network television in the United States of America one can hear a voice-over in a commercial for erectile dysfunction informing the target audience, presumably families headed for church, returning from church, or not going to church, that an erection lasting more than four hours should be regarded a medical emergency? Would you rather be kicked in the head by a horse or a bull? Do bulls in fact kick as horses do? Would you be unsettled a bit if someone said to you, "Hey, I'm going down to the Brain Tumor Treatment Center for just a bit and I'll stop by later tonight"?

What does "It just goes to show you" mean? Have you ever built or operated a trebuchet? If you could get ahold of some dynamite for recreational purposes, would you be hesitant, indifferent, or eager? Do you have a specific length shorts must be or are you flexible in this regard? Is Santa Claus in your view essentially a pedophile? How long would it take you to get over a house fire that destroyed everything you owned and thought dear to you? At what age does a fawn stop sitting in your lap and acting like a house cat or a dog and become a deer, and why does this change necessarily obtain? If you heard someone say "In America, one word says it all," what would you expect the word to be?

What is the name of the last person with whom you enjoyed sleeping? What things or people would you use the word *hardy* to describe? Do you understand how whether baseball players use steroids or not is a matter for the United States Congress to attend? Do you comprehend exactly how more casualties on a battlefield can be said to render previous casualties on a battlefield not to have been in vain? Is the argument beneath this logic not that the losing dead are worse off than the winning dead?

Is there any hope? Do we need galoshes? Are bluebirds perfect? Is there charity? Can there be reason? Does a kitten settle your nerves? Would you like to play a board game? If you would, do you know which one you'd like to play? In all of human history, would you say mothers or fathers are the more loved?

If you could see a large-animal trainer mauled in the middle of his or her show, perhaps even killed, would you prefer to see the mauling done by a lion, a tiger, or a bear? If it were a bear, would the pleasure or horror you took from the moment be mitigated or heightened in any way by the presence of bicycle-riding in the show? Is semaphore still used at sea or has it been displaced by the digital age? Would you take final pleasure if acquitted of a serious charge or would you always feel tainted? Do you see the exact humor in "That's so funny I forgot to laugh"? Does it change things a bit for you to perceive that these questions want you bad? And that they are perhaps independent of me, to some degree? That they are somewhat akin to, say, zombies of the interrogative mood?

DO YOU EVER THINK you hear someone saying "Lift-off!"? What would it mean if you dreamed you found two baby squirrels and asked two women if they knew a good baby-squirrel formula and when you fetched the squirrels you found they had drowned because you had inexplicably iced them down, and the ice had melted, and now the baby squirrels were sodden gray puppy-looking short-haired turds in a foul juice, and you broke down crying in front of the women, asking, "Why would I have *iced* them?" Do you try to listen to classical music but feel you don't ever really advance past knowing it's better than it sounds? Would any particular failing on your part today be more painful than all other failings?

Would it require more energy than you have in order for you to really lose it, or do you think really losing it can be a function of having too little energy to prevent losing it? Do the people you do not wish to talk to far exceed the number you do wish to talk to? Do you have much to say to even those to whom you do wish to speak? Do you know where it went wrong with you? Do you own any good copper? Are you favorably disposed to American Indian causes but less so if you must say Native American causes? Are you more at ease in a veneer of civilization or in a true hardwood of barbary? What is your favorite piece of equipment on a playground? Do you know by sight and sound an oboe from a bassoon? When you hear someone say "There'll be hell to pay," do you assume generally that there will be or won't be hell to pay?

Don't you think it a fairly prudent plan if in the halcyon early days of a relationship, before they've become the good old days of a relationship, one were to periodically say, "I'm sorry," and, to the reasonable response of the other party, who asks, "For what?" because one has ostensibly done nothing wrong, to say, "For everything," meaning of course everything that will accrue, as surely as the tides bring barnacles, to convert the early halcyon days into the good old days of the relationship? Do you see any value, I mean to say, in the preemptive-strike apology when times are good before they are bad? Would it delay the accumulation of the barnacles by a second or a minute or two, an hour, a day, a week, a year? Or might it be better to say right in the flush of new-intimate ecstasy, "Look, this is bound to rotten up, probably at my hand, good-bye"?

Have you read as much Samuel Johnson as you should have? Can you always immediately recall that Darwin's first name is Charles? Do you take pills you are not precisely sure you can identify? Do you feel no better, better, or inordinately better after you polish something? Are you aware that up to a third of the tongue can be removed and it, the tongue, can regenerate itself more or less completely? What is the color you most enjoy in lipstick? If you are presented a nipple with a ring through it in a sexual situation, is your first move to bite the ring itself, or to take the ring in whole, or to do something else altogether, like run?

Would you say "pine-needle green" or "green as pine needles"? If you were to be put into a primitive situation without power in a more or less temperate climate and were offered a lifetime supply of ice or fire, not to say that you could not by natural circumstance periodically gather one or the other as you found it, would you accept the ice or the fire? Doesn't it seem as if the board game called Chinese checkers was once popular and has now disappeared? What would be your best-case scenario for your being forced, or able, to say, "I accept the lash!" If you wear eyeglasses, how many times a day do you wash them? Have you lived in more houses than you've had dogs and cats? Would you like to be on a submarine? Do you have a position on pantyhose?

Do you love buffalo as much as I? May I tell you that I love buffalo and do not think you could love them as much as I love them? Have you ever seen finches or sparrows on a tree that suggest fleas or lice on a large animal? Under what circumstances would you kill yourself, and what means might you use? What do you think about a small candy factory in Desoto, Georgia, called the Desoto Nut House that once allowed tours of its kitchen while large black women handled great slabs of peanut brittle and other confections on marble tables, all of this in a sweet open warm friendly air of business and pleasure, and you emerge and buy a bag or two of nuts or candy more out of good feeling and cheer than out of any affection for the stuff, so fun was the kitchen and watching the women turn the dangerous boluses of hot sugar, and now when one goes to the Desoto Nut House one is not allowed in the kitchen because tours are no longer allowed for reasons relating to insurance? What I mean to ask is, is it not the kernel of the demise of the world as we knew it that you can no longer watch candy be made "for insurance reasons"? Does not someone need to stand up and say, "If I cannot have people watch my candy be made, as I have done for forty years without incident, because of insurance, I will not have insurance"?

Have you been to India and seen lingam coming out of the ground, and if you have, do you recall if they are only in holy places or are they also in secular places? Have you ever witnessed elephant foot maintenance? Do you know any apparently very healthy people to have died suddenly from stroke? Will you maneuver to procure very good coffee, or for you is coffee coffee? Whom do you regard as a bona fide intellectual, and have you known personally anyone you regard as a bona fide intellectual? Do you suppose that once a bird knows how to fly he pretty much can expect to fly without incident, more or less as, say, we walk about, or would you think bird flying to be fraught with aeronautical accident? How accurately can you shoot a rubber band? Have you ever been bitten by a horse? When you buy clothes, do you assiduously check the way they fit you, or do you just decide they fit or they don't and be done with it?

Do you ever hold hands with anyone? If you do not, are there circumstances in which you might hold hands with anyone? If there were a gun case full of guns, yours or someone else's, and one of the guns was dirty and fouled from use while the others were meticulously clean, would you want to see that the one gun got cleaned? If you were at a landfill and saw a large pile of girly magazines, which you do not customarily look at, beside a large pile of unopened tins of Skoal, which you have never used, would you go over there and take a pinch of snuff and have a look at a magazine? Do buzzards give you the creeps? Have you ever constructed a sandbox? If you once owned a slide rule and do not have it now, do you know what happened to it?

When was the last time you saw an ostrich? In what kinds of weather do you most like to walk? Do you enjoy oiling things or is that best left to others? Do you know what comes after "Patty cake, patty cake, baker's man / bake me a cake as fast as you can"? Are you familiar with the sport of kite fighting? Do you think of there being a proper point in your debilitation as you age at which you should, if you can, kill yourself?

Do you have any experience with boils? When people are weeping and fretting about you, do you console or attempt to move away as politely as possible? Do you find Mary Martin in *Peter Pan* sexually stimulating? Have you ever had cockles? Does Ireland sound like your kind of place or like someone else's kind of place? Have you ever been exposed to rigorous mathematical proofs, and if so, do you like them? Do you know the term for the kind of trowel, used in applying certain adhesives, that has teeth on its edge so that glue is laid down in fine rows instead of as a film?

Does any confusion arise if you see or hear pinecone and cornpone together? Do you have any impulse to wish that everything you own could somehow without overmuch trauma be made to disappear? If you had to threaten someone with either "I'mone slap the taste out of your mouth" or "I'mone knock you into next week," which colorful expression would you prefer? If someone threatened you with either of these utterances, would you rather reply "Well, pack your lunch" or "You and whose army?"

THESE SMALL BIRDS FLITTING about the top of the pine tree outside my window that I likened to fleas or lice on a large animal—may I say now more accurately that they look like gnats around the head and eyes of a tall creature? Did they get to the bottom of what has killed all the amphibians the world over? Do you think the heyday of hair spray was the 1960s, or has it lived on? Are Kotex still worn on belts? Were you ever familiar enough with gladiators that you preferred one style of combat over others—the net and trident, say, over the short sword? What sort of boat do you fancy best? Would you rather have to deal with a regulatory commission or a codes inspector? Do you have much patience for sanding wood? Have you come over time to think that you know more now than you did when young, know less now than when young, know now there is so much more to know than you knew there was to know when young that it is moot whether you think you knew more then than now or less, or do you now know that you never knew anything at all and never will and only the bluster of youth persuaded you that you did or would?

Do you keep a neat living place or a messy place? Is it better to work in a messy place and get a lot of work done or a neat place and get nothing done? Do you recall the last time you set something on fire that you were not supposed to set on fire? Do you trust or mistrust people who say "Candy is too sweet for me"? If you had to perform a field amputation to save someone's life, could you? Do you like ivory? Do you remember those children's beads that popped apart and were held together by means of stems and balls and sockets of the same material the beads were made of? Does honey come out of the front end or the back end of a bee?

Are you aware of a more likable kind of person than yourself that you would like to be like? What for you are the characteristics that make a person extremely likable? Have you ever been lain on by a heavy naked person in a boat as it raced by another boat full of heavy naked people? Is the world through with worrying about Communism? Have you known anyone to say "biscuit" in referring to a vagina? Do you subscribe to the position that there is good plastic and bad plastic? Would you rather be a bear who is compelled to eat a hundred dying salmon to make it through the winter or a salmon who has to make it past the bear to spawn and rot and die? Are small green rubber army men still sold? Would you say that civilization is protocol, a set of protocols large and smaller nesting inside each other like those Russian dolls? And that as long as the smaller protocols are followed—the trees in the forest as it were—no one much minds that the large protocol, the forest as it were, might be going to hell? Have you ever been not disappointed by a banana split? If a voice instructed you that the tub of salve levitating over the table before you was invisible cream and invited you to put some on and join the party, would you put the cream on? Would you prefer a child who says "I want one" or one who says "That's bad" when told in answer to her question "What's a slave?" that "It's a person who has to do anything you want it to do"? Do you know the Lindy rhythm? Are you any good at horseshoes? How fast do the fastest birds fly?

In mustard, do you fancy the fancy or the ballpark? When part of a group, do you favor stepping to the rear or to the fore? Do you know enough about rifles to select one for purchase? Would you think it improbable that a man might be a professional trainer of military and police dogs and also a certified instructor of yoga? I mean to say, is that avocational yoking not unlike having a meal of hamburger and tofu? As you age, do you find you enjoy driving in cars less or more? Do you have the patience or the fortitude for house painting? Would you mind telling me in detail what your proficiency in the realm of sewing is?

Do you regard yourself a person who has money, a person who is going to have money, or a person who has no money and, barring an accident, is not going to have any money? Who is the best guitar player in the world, in your view? If it had to be the case that a raccoon, a skunk, a possum, or an otter was going to take up residence under your bed, which one would you prefer it be? Do you know what actuaries are? Would the phrase "clapping cancer" mean anything to you? Do you enjoy the ineptitude of local news broadcasters or are you annoyed by it? Do you enjoy the slick professionalism of national news broadcasters or are you annoyed by it? Do you know an anole from a gecko and a skink? Can you love, still? Did you ever love? Is there heartbreak in rain, or cheer? Are you tired?

DO YOU DO YARD sales? Are you happy with your teeth? Do you in general trust or mistrust earnestness? Do you attend parades? Do you gamble? Do you like pull candy? Have you any weapons on you at the moment? Would you buy a pearl choker? Are you important? Do you have any skin disabilities such as eczema or psoriasis? Can you envision saying seriously to someone, "You just holler for help, and I'll come arunnin'"? Do you like to use terms like "triangulation" and "extrapolation" when not speaking mathematically? Are you bold, would you say? Can you count in languages other than your mother tongue? Would you like for your life to be more, or less, dangerous than it is? Have you ever experienced any sort of hernia? Is baseball all it's cracked up to be? Do people stink, mostly? Is there life on other planets, or after death on this one, as it were? Do you like stalling for time? Can you lob a grenade accurately, would you think? Are there interstices in your character?

Is it hard for you to resist the demands of whiny people? Have you ever wound an armature for an electric motor? Do you know precisely what a chilblain is? Do you bite your tongue or grind your teeth at night? Have you ever witnessed any credible sign of ghosts? Do you read a newspaper to discover what is going on or for other reasons? If you were now thirteen again, what would you do that you did not do when you were thirteen the first time, and what would you not do that you did? Do you own Allen wrenches? Does it seem to you that the phenomenon of people secretly drinking on the job has virtually disappeared? Have you ever dropped something like a box of books out a third-story window and found its impact inordinately funny? Do you prefer loose pants, to the point of slovenliness, or tight pants, to the point of dapperness? Are you thrilled by new automotive concepts? Can you execute a one-handed cartwheel?

What period of history most interests you? If someone knocked on your door and handed you the leash to a large standard poodle and said it was yours, would you resist or acquiesce in the receipt of this animal? Would you rather see a clown act at the circus predicated on cartoon violence or see a big cat get in a good swipe at the lion tamer and cut him badly? Do you recall the moment you first rode a bicycle? Do you actually handle bullies or do you just know what is to be done with bullies but don't do it? Do you use any glue to hand or are you made nervous by not having the correct glue for this or that repair? Do you know the names of your first three lovers?

Why do plants and trees rot agreeably but animals rot so disagreeably? What today would make you cry? Are you sure your relatives like you? Do you still use the word *retarded*? Are you interested in military history more than your reading in or knowledge of military history might suggest? What do you think of when you hear the term "strap-on"? Do you know the literal translation of *bas relief*, and do you know if there is any other sort of relief? Do you have long-range plans for self-improvement or have you about given up in that area? Would you rather lift weights until you sweat or sit in a sauna until you sweat? Do you favor any sort of cracker over other crackers?

Would you prefer to spend a day at a mental hospital or a day at a mall? The jewelry called turquoise— is that the original noun, correctly used, from which the color turquoise has been appropriated, similar to the appropriation of "gold"? Do you know any outright buffoons? Can you take apart a clothes dryer and get it going right? Do you know what bean futures are? Would you say there is anything you care passionately about? Can you imagine accurately certain smells— say, the smell of cedar? Are you preintellectual, anti-intellectual, intellectual, or postintellectual? Would you have a life with sugar cane and a mule and land, or a life with an apartment and some cans of soup and a phone? Do you know what the phrase "turtle head" means when used so: "My sister was standing under the hoop not moving because she said she had a turtle head"? May I tell you that the author of that sentence illustrating turtle head is not me and I don't know who the author is? Do you use facial cleansers with abradant particles in them? Do you enjoy hockey? Are there circumstances in which you would take off your clothes in public, excluding their being on fire? Do you find black lipstick attractive? Have you ever worn any "moleskin" pads against corns? Would you be interested in having a deglanded skunk as a pet?

Did you know that when a cow is slaughtered you want it stunned, but not dead, from the time you raise it by a chain on one rear leg (you'll be dodging the other three) and swing the cow over a drain and cut its jugulars or carotids by quick vertical slashes to the throat that release gallons of blood, the ready falling out of the cow and pumping out of the cow of which is chiefly why you want the cow not dead but stunned, and that as this blood pours forth the cow enters a deepening sleeplike state, its heart continuing to pump, its muscles continuing to contract, its legs thrashing less violently, all of which is important for the blood to be able to keep exiting, and that well after the blood has trickled to a stop, when the skinned head is put in a rack for a pathology inspection, the facial muscles will be crawling as if rather large worms are at work in the face?

Do you like estate sales? Do you know what kind of acreage one would have to plant in coffee in order to produce enough coffee just for one's own consumption, or if such a venture might be feasible? Should a girl be discouraged from bra stuffing? Do you know why or how, and to what extent, trucking has replaced rail shipping? If you saw on a T-shirt the slogan BLOOD IS LIKE A PARACHUTE, what would you think that slogan intends to mean? Are there means of determining how accurate one's oven thermostat is other than by incorporating an after-market oven thermometer, the accuracy of which itself may need proofing? Am I wasting your time? Are you wasting mine? Can life be viewed as time wasting and time not wasting? Do the not wasters prove better off than the wasters? Are the wasters liabilities or are they assets to the not wasters? If a man is running a ninety-degree grinder and it catches his pants and torques into him and he sees blood coming through his jeans at the crotch and he says "Hmmm," and puts the grinder down and sits on the bumper of his truck and lights a cigarette before investigating what is wrong in his pants, and before heading to the ER, is he, would you say, wasting time or not? Do you know what culottes are?

WHAT POWER MAGNIFICATION DO you like in a binocular? Have you ridden those electric buses that connect to cables over the street by means of a rig similar to that used by bumper cars at the fair and that can come untracked and so have to be put back on track by the driver using nonconductive ropes tied to the contact rig? Do you like hanging file folders? If I invited you now to drive around in a bright red car on this bright day, would you like to come? Do you regard a particular day of the week as sinister? Is *revolted* a word you use without irony? When you envision restoring the world to any of its better former states, do wolves figure into your visions? Do you like it when people sing "Happy Birthday" to you?

To be an anarchist, properly speaking, does one need to actively undo government or may one just passively not participate? Do you know of or perhaps own any dead trees that you are particularly fond of and wish to see stand for longer yet? Is the charge that manufacturing a Puerto Rican Barbie is racist mitigated or not by the fact that Puerto Rican girls are wild for Puerto Rican Barbie and indifferent to white Barbie? Have you ever had to maintain a swimming pool for your mother, and if so, did this job reduce your fondness for swimming in pools and perhaps for pools themselves?

May I tell you that I once knew a refrigerator man, who called them simply "boxes," who would come to my house if I poked a hole in the Freon lines trying to defrost the freezer with an ice pick, and fix the hole with epoxy he mixed right there on the bottom of a Coke bottle, and who once brought his assistant Burgess with him and after the repair had been effected said to me, "Now, we know you smart, you go to college, and we wanting to ax you a question, because you smart, you go to college, and . . ." and went on like that until I said, "All right, Nevada, I'm not smart but we'll say I'm smart, what is the question?" and Nevada said, "Well, Burgess's pennis don't get hard, and we wondering if you could recommend something for Burgess's pennis to get hard," and Burgess offered up as proof of his lost virility a brief testament that before this debilitation had obtained one could hear him bust a nut, as he put it, for blocks on Beaver Street in Jacksonville, Florida, where they knew I was from, and that so moved was I by their appeal to my eminent authority and by the pronunciation *pennis* and by Burgess's obvious anguish—he was wringing his hands at the red kitchen table—that I stepped without hesitation to the cabinet and withdrew my

Bob Hoffman Protein Powder for weight lifters and mixed some of it with a honey-and-vinegar cocktail over ice and told Burgess to drink it all at once, and he did, and shortly said he thought he felt something, and then said he was sure he felt something, positive he felt something, and his soaring spirits lifted him away from the table and Nevada carried him on to his appointment with virility? Would it matter in your decision to accept it or not whether the large standard poodle brought to your door and offered to you was white or black, and whether it had the fancy haircut or not?

Would you prefer to expire on a fair day or foul, or do you think you'll be past appreciating and lamenting the weather by that point? Can you handle honey without getting it on your fingers? Do you know if the Japanese Zero was actually painted chrome yellow or did it for some ahistorical reason appear in that color in the American polystyrene models later made of it? Do you know the names of your great-grandparents? Would you stand a better chance of hitting a long-legged bird with a bolo or with a boomerang? Are you a connoisseur of chocolate, or is your appetite for it unrefined? Can you lay up a basketball? Do you like starch in your clothes? Do you favor any one form of sexual congress over others? Do you prefer hyperactive children or slow children? How far will you walk to procure a daily newspaper? Can you successfully hit the Close Door and Open Door buttons on elevators in time? Do you have any interest in being in a terrorist organization, and if so, which one appeals to you as having the most justified mission? At what point is a gosling a goose?

Do you go in for the tall tale? Do you own any leotards? Are you familiar with the term "the fancy"? Can you spit well? Are you bothered when a popular local weatherman is dismissed for sexual dalliance in a public restroom? Did you have an aunt or an uncle of whom you were more fond than your other relatives? Do you understand when you can cook on copper and when you cannot? Knowing what you might about construction, if you had to build a bridge or dig a tunnel of equal length, which would you prefer? What do you think was the gentlest, sanest civilization in history? If you could transport to a past civilization, which one would it be? What breed of chickens attracts you most? In sexual attraction, is there a feature or set of features that you find is a deal maker or a deal breaker?

Has it occurred to you at some point that you are a whole lot less gifted than you might have once thought yourself, in one or in several aspects of your youness, or have you maintained a more or less steady assessment of your abilities and talents and indeed of your worth? Is your ass inordinately chapped by television chefs who in your view cannot cook, or are you amused by them, or are you as indifferent to them as to other pretenders about you?

Isn't the weather nice today? Is there anyone whom you've been thinking about calling for some time for no really good reason so that if you do call you'll have to explain yourself as just assenting to a whim? Do you like it when people to whom you've done no wrong arrange themselves to be done with you? Would you rather be a lumberjack, a plumber, or a croupier? Do you like to handle lead? Have you ever pinned butterflies? In tennis, do you favor a lot of topspin or do you like a flat ball? Have you been so thirsty that you've drunk questionable untreated water? Have you heard that water buffalo are more dangerous than tigers and lions and elephants? Was prom-going fun or a misery for you? Would you like, right now, some cornbread?

ARE YOU FAMILIAR WITH the economics term "elasticity of demand"? Does the prospect of a vacation tire you out? Do you know a rasp from a file? Have you ever gone out the window or the emergency door of a bus? Have you hunted ducks, and if so, did you use decoys, and if so, did the decoys seem to make the hunting unfair? Would you be more interested in the murder of one chocolatier by another chocolatier than in the murder of one jockey by another jockey? Is there a profession the murder of one member of which by another would interest you more than all other intraprofessional murders? Is there a category of interprofessional murder that would interest you more than others?

Do you sometimes find some appeal, as opposed to your customary cynical derision of the idea, in the notion of issuing a Cry for Help? If a good friend said to you "I've never really been happy," apparently in earnest, would you laugh? Would you have anticipated that Jack LaLanne would outlive Buddy Ebsen? If you were to be confined in close quarters with it, would you prefer a horse, a mule, or a donkey? Do you have a tattoo? Do you use the terms "alloyed" and "unalloyed"? How do you hold with corporal punishment of children? Would a long view through space and time of human history on the earth resemble the compressed photography you may have seen of maggots working a corpse?

Do you know the difference when they are on the wing between a gull and a tern? What are the factors that influence your selection of automobile tires? How many times can you recall as a child eating a good-sized spoonful of dirt? Do you prefer being colder than you wish to be or hotter than you wish to be? If you were from this moment on to be known by any two-name combination of these names—Alice, Emily, Katherine, Sveta, Bruiser, Frank, Gerard, Tyrone— what would your new name be? Do you know who invented Velcro, and when? Do you know how many human lives there have been, including the present batch, and whether the present number alive exceeds the number alive at any time in the past? Have you ever packed your own wheel bearings? What do you do when you get to feeling really low?

If you did play marbles as a child, do you know rings, pig's eye, what is meant by "dates," and so forth?

Have you been responsible for the death of a songbird? Do you shine your shoes? Does the phrase "rampart standard" mean anything to you? Is there a candy bar you like over others? Why do "making hay" and "haymaker" have substantially different meanings? Does "bimbo" refer only to women? How would you, on impulse, fill this in: "We got to get us some [blank] down heah"? How about "crispins and lardons"? If you heard of a "chiropractic boondoggle," what would you think that might involve?

What is the right-sized dog for you? Can you hit a golf ball? Do you like lizards? Do you use the word *spatial*? Have you ever seen or tried the old sport paddleball, which used very heavy plywood paddles? Did you ever or do you now own a set of French curves? Are you aggressive and with it on money, or passive and out of it? Do you like movies? Can you recall eating crayons? If you hired a maid and she came in the first day and said, "I'll be needing me some Bab-o and Skinner's Raisin Bran and for you to get out of my way," would you think you had made a very good hire, or would the bluster worry you? Would such a maid be the kind you need to make pencil marks on the liquor-bottle labels for, or not? Have you ever seen actual police photos of a crime scene with a corpse in it? Do you sometimes just make up your mind and set out to Have a Very Good Day and not let anything deflect you from doing just that? Will you eat birthday-candle wax on the icing of a cake or do you meticulously pick it out?

Do you think you yourself could make anything out of birch bark? Are you more likely to purchase something calling itself a salve or something calling itself a balm, and are you more drawn to it or less drawn to it if it is in a tin, as opposed to, let's say, in a tube? If you could be an assassin or an ice-cream manufacturer, which would it be? Are you conversant with wildflowers? When you see public officials, do you see trajectories of menace or do you see public servants doing their best? Does what the Germans did to the Jews, next to what the Americans did to the Indians, differ largely only in the efficiency of the Germans and the inefficiency of the Americans? Have you ever had and really enjoyed cold fountain Pepsi-Cola over shaved ice early in the morning? Would you like something like a little cold Pepsi and a good recreational drug right now? What percentage of people in general would you say are so stupid or misled or just altogether so fucked up in the head that we would be better off if they were not present at all? Do you use throw rugs in your house? Would you ever buy a significant pet, by which I mean something more substantial than a mouse or a fish, from a pet shop as opposed to from a breeder or otherwise less retail purveyor? Do you recall the nice ivory color of a jawbreaker as the red coating wears off, and the nice porcelain knocking sound you can effect with the jawbreaker and your teeth? Do you think there might be a snake equivalent of some sort to the Christmas bird count? Will one hyena stand and fight a dog? Were you any good at Flyback? Is there any circumstance in which you would allow yourself to be addressed as "Skipper"? If someone you knew vaguely called you up and said, "I can do the dirty dog all night long, you want to go out with me?" what would you say?

Was Luther's declamation called the Diet of Worms, or did that refer to the convention that drew it up? If it was the proclamation, would you rather issue a Diet of Worms or issue a papal bull? How often do you burn toast? What do you suppose is the ratio in the world of underweight people to overweight people? Do you think that tropical fish and birds are as content as they appear to be in their tanks and cages? Do you know why it is that freedom is not free? Would it be correspondingly true, if freedom is not free, that captivity is not captive? If you were to help a child enter himself into a soapbox derby contest, would you prefer it be the life-size race or the model competition? Do you know why the two forms of this soapbox-derby business exist? Do you have a fondness for operating a small outboard motor on calm water early in the morning, over operating that motor at any other time of day? Have you used the word *splendid* without irony? Do you think a man named Chocolate could be elected governor of any state other than California? Have you known people who loosen their clothing for the purpose of sitting around? Have you ever witnessed a serious fireworks accident either to persons or to property? Would you rob a bank?

Are you tardy more than not? Do you picnic, and do you use a basket if you do? Can you say for sure that you have loved? Are you looking forward to retirement? Does the recovery of the alligator, they say nearly extinct in the 1960s, surprise you? How many one-armed men do you know, or women? What are the chances that you could have been an astronaut?

Do you like paint? Is there a future? Do you need support clothing of any sort? Do you like to report that you are alarmed? Do you like it when others report they are alarmed? Will you buy from a meat market whose slogan is "Nobody beats our meat"? Is mass a function of weight or weight a function of mass? Can you sharpen your knives and scissors or are you dependent upon others for sharpening? Do you know why the pleated paper cups for cupcakes do not burn? Is a bruise a contusion, or is a bruise a manifestation of a contusion? If you soaked a good-sized rolled-up newspaper and dropped it, say, ten stories onto the street, how large do you think the newsprint would spread out on impact? Are you familiar with the bird species todies? Are you amused when you hear a girl say "This sucks my dick," meaning she is disgusted by something? Why does a split in a fingernail transmit itself apparently forever? Is it natural that those much taken with themselves young become less so as they age, and those not so taken young become more confident of themselves later?

Are you familiar with the spring-loaded stinging mechanism of the jellyfish and other things in the ocean you'd better not touch, perhaps called nematocyst? Would you think that your vocabulary shrinks, expands, or holds constant over time? If one man suggested to a second that he resembled Ted Kennedy, and the second in protest said, "I ain't got no outside gorilla," what would his remark mean? Are you drawn to bowling and the ambience of bowling? Does it strike you as odd or not odd that shooting enthusiasts commonly shoot discarded bowling pins in timed competitions to see who can shoot them off a table the fastest? Have you ever read Virgil? Do you think in terms of calculus? Can you wade across a stream with some speed and depth to it without falling down, usually?

Do you like crickets? Are you sane? Does the moon's rising or the sun's setting do it for you more? Can you abide horse thievery? Have you purchased the services of a prostitute? What's it like when you first wake up? Is there an aftertaste to a cigarette, or is it all the immediate taste of the cigarette? When do the stars render themselves most visible? Can we say with certainty that we are free? What's it like being you? Does Carole Lombard stir you in any way? If good fences make good neighbors, what kind of fence in your view makes the best neighbor? Would you like to have right now any particular kind of candy? Has any part of you ever herniated or prolapsed? Do you doodle much? Do you prefer a cloth to a paper napkin? Can you hold your liquor? Do you think Charles Lindbergh was a good fellow or a cad? If a place is infested with feral cats, is it okay in your book to shoot them? Can you tell me why now at this minute I see in my mind the time I picked up on my paddle a large gray rat snake as she swam across the Flint River in Georgia and she hissed at me gently? What is the opposite of a "strapping lad"? Will we be struck down in heaven? Can we hope for a better tomorrow? Do we have the look of heroes to anyone? Can we be better or worse than we are? Do you have anything you'd like to say?

WOULD YOU CHECK IN for a long stay, a short stay, or would you not stay at all at The Hotel Enema? Would you be interested in getting in a car with girls who are chewing gum and excited about going to the beach? Are you more subject to periods of psychological fragility in the morning than in the evening? If Julia says, "Jacques and I are vegetarians," and Jacques says, "But we eat meat, too," and Julia then says, "We eat everything," is this amusing to you or inane? In your family history is there any mention of an aging relative throwing feces at a grandchild? Do you enjoy seeing airplanes write with smoke in the sky? Would you prefer to see the earth flood or burn totally up? Do you favor any particular kind of fountain? Do you get satisfaction from wrapping up a bag of garbage and getting it out of the house? Do you like to make stock? Do you have a rivet gun or a hot-glue gun? Would you say your man is Dickens or Trollope? Have you ever counted tree rings? Would you rather spend time with gangsters, with pornographers, or with professional dancers? Do you wonder why if there is, say, vanilla Coke and cherry Coke, and if the global market is the thing, why there is not, say, nutmeg Coke and cumin Coke and anise Coke and garlic Coke and sauerbraten Coke and horseradish Coke and chili Coke and coconut Coke and lemongrass Coke? Have you lost your mind?

Do you like to dance in the rain in your tight underwear? Do you hawk phlegm? Is there a number of children that should never be exceeded in your immediate presence? Does the term "bogolusian" mean anything to you? If you found yourself in a bull ring with a bull in it, would you start running immediately or would you wait until the bull took an interest in you and base your move on his? Would you drink something called a "plumber's concoction"? Would you object to any part of your person or character or any part of your behavior being called dainty? Is the idea of living in a shack attractive? Can you abide red wrigglers, or do you prefer the solid sandy gravity of a good, thick earthworm? Would a vegetarian who objects to meat on moral grounds be able to participate with a clear conscience in prescribed burning of forests? Do birds defecate from aloft when in established flight? Can a car body not be made of copper? Have you taken game from artificially confined populations of it, such as are on hunting plantations and in trout ponds? What is the age past which you do not wish to see someone naked? Do you fancy watercress?

Do you like it when your body is sore? Had you the opportunity, would you attend clown school? Will you linger to see a sunset more readily than you might get up to see a sunrise? Do you consider yourself a charitable person or an essentially selfish and self-protective person? Do you understand the physics of chocolate? If you were laying siege to a walled town and could lob in a ton of something, what would you lob in? If you were in the town, what would you most not want to see come flying in? Should the answers to the two previous questions be the same? Is most talk idiocy?

Are you familiar with the cow pea, and do you find them difficult to locate? Do you know the origin and the meaning of the chevron? Do tools of any particular sort attract you? Would you like to have been seen naked when you weren't naked at points in your life you can recall? Would you say that for you population control is not an issue, or that it is an issue but you have no suggestions, or that it is an issue and you have suggestions? If you have population-control suggestions, what are they? Do you find the rimless centerfire cartridge more menacing-looking than the rimmed rimfire? Do you feel protective in an unusual way of the turkey oak?

Has your experience with bankers been positive, in general? How often do you go for an undirected walk? If you could be made taller nonsurgically, would you go for it? If you were part of a pilot/gunner team on an aircraft, which position would you prefer? Is the chief function of the doily protective or decorative or both? Do you know what is signified by "boomlay," possibly "a boomlay"? Would you eat toe soup? If told your house was to be painted either "arsenical green" or "cupric yarng," which would you pick? Do you synchronize all your clocks? If so, are they set correctly, fast, or slow? Have you ever taken a beating? Would you like one?

If you find an unopened stick of Juicy Fruit gum on the sidewalk, will you chew it? Do you talk to squirrels? Do you like to passionately argue for a position or an outcome or a gain of any sort about which itself you are indifferent? Do you lick stamps or envelopes with your tongue or wet them less directly?

Are you familiar with the joke in which billeting is sought for "a hundred soldiers without Peters"? When a trellis collapses, with a rose on it, do you cut back the rose or keep the rose entire as you rebuild the trellis and tie the rose back up? Have you ever seen an owl so large you mistook it for a man in a sport coat sitting in a tree? Is there anything better than snow outside and fire inside? Can you identify tuille? Would you rather play a board game with a child all day or go over Niagara Falls in a barrel? Have you ever fished with niblet corn? Do you care for Laurel and

Hardy? If you were to be incarcerated in a mental institution, would you care where it was and what kind of place it was? Do you collect your old license tags? Are you partial to peppermint, and if so, do you best like it in soap, in candy, or in a pie? Do you know how gyroscopes function aeronautically? Do you have the patience to upholster a chair? Are you big on pudding? Is a catfish likely to get more sympathy from you than a fish with scales? Between the fox-trot and the waltz, at which are you better? Could Oswald have done it alone? Are you familiar with the joke that features a female soda jerk asking a boy brandishing two new toy pistols, "Do you want your nuts crushed?"

Will you be taking a constitutional today, perhaps thinking fondly of your beloved? Will storm clouds not fret your brow? Have you ever built a boat, or a model boat? Do you die in your dreams? Do you shop credit-card offers for lower interest rates and higher rewards? Have you eaten dung? Does the prospect of going to Africa instill in you any willies? Do you find the three-legged milking stool charming? The three-legged dog?

Would you watch cricket all afternoon before you would watch ice hockey? Do you have aspirations for things getting better? Are these things, if you do have aspirations for their getting better, specific or vague? If you do not have aspirations for things getting better, did you once? If you do not have aspirations for things getting better but did once, can you say what ended your aspirations for things getting better? Have you ever made car payments? Do you have life insurance? Do you know the suicide clauses of your life-insurance policy, if you have one? Have you ever seen lava flow? Would you like to be momentarily in a jail cell with a man who keeps repeating that he does not take survivors or take no for an answer? Would you like to eat soft-serve ice cream beside a municipal pond colored that fetid green from goose shit and paddled upon by uncivil ducks? Would you like to go to a stock-car race? If she's dead, would you like to send word to your mother? Do you ever say to yourself, "Lay me down to sleep"? Doesn't that have the nicest little music to it?

Now that we near the end, do you find yourself swelling with misgiving? Did you say enough smart things and few enough harebrained, and did you stand up and fight at least once? Did you live rooted or were you off your pins all the livelong day? Do you blame your failures on yourself, on someone else, or on no one at all? Is it jelly you like, smooth and easy, or is it preserves with that tincture of grit? Is you stupid, do you think?

ARE YOU SURE OF yourself? Do you use the word *co-ordinates*? Does a snifter of brandy—swirling, amber, bright, piquant—strike you as a handsome thing? Is there trouble in Paradise? Do wheels have fun? Can there be surcease in the pursuit of charity? Would the number of snake teeth there have been in time exceed or equal or be less than the number of human teeth, do you think? Will you ride a pony? Can a man's or a woman's becoming a hero be an accident? Can you imagine doing something in your life that will be fully satisfying and redeeming for your having tried to do it, whether you succeeded in it or failed, and that, correspondingly, would be fully shameful had you not tried to do it? If a boy is robbed and shot delivering a pizza, has his life been a waste? Are you more likely to have occasion, do you think, to say "billets-doux" or "pietà"?

Would you rather be regular army or army reserve? If you were, or are, a woman, would you rather have trouble or women's trouble, medically speaking?

Do you know the principles of pruning? Are you wary of botulism? Would you rather see a cancan show or a turtle race? Could you be intimate with a blind person? Do you like a waiter who doesn't write orders or are you irritated by the affectation of it? Is your mind bubbling pablum or snails commingling? Would you be disturbed to hear a child say, "The best thing about Granny is where she is"? Would you be more disturbed or less disturbed, provided you were disturbed at all, were the child who said this your own? Would you comb a mule? Would you wear a prosthetic testicle or breast? Would you run for public office? Would you sit outside the Sorbonne on a bench wearing a beret? Do you eat beetroot? Were you a bird and could choose, would you be white or black? Is bacon for you nasty or sublime? Would you have trouble killing in combat, do you think? Does the prospect of hernia bother you more than might other more severe and more likely medical disorders? If you learned that you were vying within a love triangle with a Navy SEAL, would you be concerned? Could you be depended upon, in a love triangle with a SEAL, to down a goodly quaff of schnapps and say, "He might outkill me but he shan't outlove me!"?

Are you fond of a tree's turning red? If you had a child who was mad for a go-cart, and pestering you to buy her one, would you spring for it? Do you believe that what is now called snail mail will disappear and be replaced entirely by electronic mail? If a person applied to you for a job, eminently qualified, and you learned in the interview that he had surrounded himself with fifty thousand images of monkeys by his own count, to include the monkey-print shirt and pants he was wearing that you could see and the monkey-print briefs he told you he was wearing, would you be less inclined to hire him than if revelation of his monkey obsession had not obtained? Do you have any idea how the name "Jujube" came about or what it might mean, if anything, apart from the eponymous candy? If you were fairly well laid up and immobile in a hospital, would you accept sexual favor from a nurse? If you accepted sexual favor from a nurse, would you be concerned about the long-term romantic complications you might not want—specifically, that the nurse might not be a purely practical professional in this respect but an impractical person getting involved with you in ways you deemed yourself not likely to reciprocate? If you accepted sexual favor from a nurse, would you be concerned about securing the door to the room and otherwise ensuring privacy, or would that be the nurse's business entirely? Do you prefer to live in a country where eating well is important or are you just as happy in a country where people are indifferent to eating well or perhaps even embrace eating badly?

Do you know how to house-train a dog? Have you ever had surgery on your tongue? Would you like more ballroom-dance skills than you now have? Are the Dry Tortugas dry? Is it Dry Tortuga? Are you afraid of country people? Do you think that an inclination to talk a lot is a sign of weakness? When a woman wears a pair of men's pajamas and removes the top, retaining the pants, do you find this a sexually stimulating outfit? Are you much good at Ping-Pong? Does having to call Ping-Pong "table tennis" strike you as an abomination not unrelated to a whole fabric of other abomination in the world that is sometimes difficult to codify and identify but which might fit loosely under the heading of global correctification? Is it the case that anyone has been forced to say table tennis rather than Ping-Pong, or am I deluded here? Are children allowed to play cowboys and Indians today? Are rubber army men still marketed? Do you recall my asking you this earlier? Does it gall you that it might be the case that rubber army men are not sold today for reasons of political marketing contraindications during a time when the production of real army men is on the increase? Would you rather operate in a headwind or a tailwind? Do you think you could make a dish to eat from pinecones? Does the noise a bullwhip makes involve breaking the sound barrier? Are there more problems in the world because of historical, linguistic, or mathematical ignorance?

What is your favorite spice? Do you enjoy bundling up in cold weather? Does it interest you that in trying to ask you if you enjoy bundling up I first wrote bumbling and bungling? Do any of my failures, or successes, large and small as they are, both, matter to you at all? What does matter to you? Could you give me, say, a three-zone general answer, and a ten-point specific list of those areas and those exact things, respectively, that you consider of importance to you? Are you disturbed by, amused by, or indifferent to the emergence in the United States of the fancy retail coffee-shop industry? Are you disturbed by, amused by, or indifferent to foul language on T-shirts and bumper stickers? Have you seen in your time good old playground equipment be removed and not be replaced or, worse, be replaced by inferior new stuff? Do you hope that airlines go out of business? Would you put your hand in the mouth of a lion or a pony first? What would you do if the doorbell rang and there stood a woman wearing a set of peach-colored underwear holding a peach-colored poodle on a leash? Would it be appropriate for either party, in the case of the woman in peach with a peach dog and your greeting this pair, to apologize for anything? Do you distinguish between the fox-trot and the waltz when you see them?

If you were told "The photographs she is preparing are designed to scare the populace" what word or phrase would most secure your interest? Similarly, what about "The Scottish horses, heavy on the ground" most piques your curiosity? If you were told you could move to a cabin in the Andes, yours for the taking and with some servants on the grounds ready to work for you and that the farm was self-sufficient with their labor, would you go? Do you recall the last time you made mud pies or took a bite of dirt? Would you anticipate that a given day of the week might have more suicides committed on it than the others? Would you anticipate that a given day of the week might have more murders committed on it than the others? If there is a day of the week higher in suicide than the other days, and a day higher in murder, would you anticipate that they might be the same day?

Do you know the Druids? Do you understand violence or are you alien to it and frightened and appalled? Do you believe in getting out the vote? Is your underwear in top condition or not top condition? What is the most you have paid for a painting? Do you get satisfaction from new tires or more satisfaction from stretching the use out of bald and "dangerous" tires? Is it correct that the New World had the cocoa but that only the Old could make chocolate? Does the number of things you are not interested in exceed the number of things you are interested in? Do you find the overcast day somewhat anesthetic and cheering and the bright day assaultive and depressing? Do you know what is meant by the term "pipe dope"?

Is light rain falling straight down more pleasing to you than a heavier rain going a bit sideways? Can you abide the poodle haircut? What would you make of finding a large dildo fitted with an ejaculatory bulb-

and-tube mechanism in an oil drum serving as a trash can in the parking lot of a liquor store? Does one's having "old stomping grounds" suggest that one once stomped on them? If, properly speaking, one did not stomp but just got by, would it not be more correct to speak of a return to one's old getting-by grounds? Is it fair to say that the world comprises those who are politicians, those who are movie stars, those who get by, and criminals? If you are walking along and see a really good stick, can you pass it up?

CAN'T YOU BE THERE when the stars explode? How daft are we? More daft, less daft, or just as daft as people were before? Would all the snow in the world truly not change the color of the pine needles? Isn't it moot to point out that someone is not a political person when we can rightfully argue that he is not even a person? If you are having troubles, can they not always be held at bay by exercising until you are tired and putting on a pair of good shoes? Can't one just snap back at the world with a little Juicy Fruit? Is your hair not what it once was? Do you find that it cannot rain enough for you, or snow enough, or blow enough? Do you find that interventionists are on the rise or in the ascendant—people, I mean, with *plans*, and by plans I mean plans they deem superior to yours? Does it occur to you more often than it once might have that you are a nebbish? Can you explain the sudden necessity should you receive, say, a prospectus and annual shareholders' report from, say, the Coca-Cola Company that you read the entire thing? Are you still living in such a way that suggests you are waiting for the real living to start at some later and unspecified date? Do you think this sense of delay or stalling would be wiped away were you told you had, say, twenty-two months to live, rock-solid certain you'll be gone in twenty-two months from, say, esophageal cancer—would you set about the *actual living* you have in theory been not yet doing? Would you go to Italy and eat well and get softer and die? Would you fly to Islamabad and enter the street and buffet along in the crowded market indifferent to what became of you? Would you fly to Australia and sit in the airport bar and drink beer? Would you call enemies and provoke them, or assuage them? Would you call old loves? Would you tend to your shoes? Would you commit crimes? Do you know the alleged benefit conferred by cucumber slices over the eyes?

Isn't it true that there is a rare kind of person who perceives, as does a good dog, that life is doing something meaningful, and who discovers what it is and goes about doing it with a spirit of moderate hustle, and there is a not rare kind of person who perceives none of this and who goes about doing what is necessary in a spirit of aggrievedness?

Have you ever noticed that pine trees bloom—whether to say they flower or not I cannot say, but they do something that looks seed-poddy and it's probably those wormlike things, I guess in clusters, like starfish or anemones somewhat, I have . . . well, just put it this way: have you ever noticed what look like flowers on pine trees? How about this: "That bird came through the forest like the shadow of a bullet"? What kind of condition are you in if what you think would improve your disposition is a thousand push-ups and a barbershop haircut with cologne and hair tonic making you reek up the place? Is it reasonable, productive, and legitimate if, within the current climate that apotheosizes goal setting as the summum bonum for proper living, one sets the goal of no goal setting?

Are you peculiar about your socks these days, or at this point are socks socks? Is it really tenable that a person has a soul, whether he has a cell phone or not, and a grasshopper does not? Do you know what it means to swage metal? Are your shoes untied more often than it seems they should be? Do you have a dour cast about you? Is your cheer false and blustery? Is it a strain to smile? Does only convention and habit and cowardice keep you from being violent?

If Jimi Hendrix walked in your room and said, "Sit tight there, popo, I shall play you one" and affected to get out his guitar, what would you do? Would you say, "Wait, Jimi. You're dead lo these forty years," or "Wait, Jimi, let me call up a friend or two—not a big party, mind you, but this is a special thing for me and I want to share it with others if it's okay with you—is that all right?" or "God, no, Mr. Hendrix, that shit would split my head open now," or "Lay some weed on me before you rip it, bro," or "Okay, Jimi, but if the police come, do not call them goofballs please"? Or "Dude! Do you realize that the counterculture for which you were such a superb herald has become so mainstream now that your prodigy is invoked to sell Pepsi-Cola?" Or "Not now. Maybe later"? Or "I was going to make a BLT, you want one?" Or "Jimi! Man, I saw a thing you could dig, on the ceiling of a gym in Montana, some graffiti that said 'There's only two things in life that makes it worth living: firm feelin women and guitars tuned good' and it did not make me think of you when I read it, but now that you are here you make me think of it. Someone had Xed over the *wo-* so it could also read 'firm feelin men.' We've opened up a bit since you were here"? Or would you say nothing to Jimi Hendrix at all? What if you said, "Play me some of that dang cock-stiffening guitar, James," realizing you did not know what his formal name was, and Jimi said, "Aw, now don't go talkin all nasty on me"? What if you suggested that you and Jimi Hendrix go outside and work on your bird count? What if you asked him if he'd ever collected baseball cards? What if his ordeal wherever he's been these forty years had made him a demon and he leaps on you and tears out one of your eyeteeth to use for a pick on this tune he purports to play for you? And you sit there holding your bloody mouth and smiling when he plays it? What if the state of having lost your mind is exactly congruent to the state of your not having lost your mind?

What if what others say suddenly makes not less sense than what you yourself say? If someone came into your home and said that for no charge he would run a Lionel model train of whatever gauge the big ones are all around the inside perimeter of your house, a quiet train that makes a gentle choo-choo cooing here and there and that might blow little puffs of smoke and that would run all the time (as demonstrators do in model train shops, perhaps you've seen these), would you tell him no or would you tell him to knock himself out and lay that Lionel down? Is there one thing in your life you regret having done (or not having done) more than anything else?

If we were walking down a pleasant street and we came to a nice old-fashioned pharmacy, perhaps with a soda fountain intact, is there anything we should go in and get? Would we be happier if we had something we do not have, or if we were told something we've not been told, or if we said something we've not said, or if we did something we've not done, or if we did not have something that we do have? Have you ever watched bats come out of a wall? How the soft, friendly things keep pouring silently out of the brick? How they have focus, and mission, and you do not? How they will not ever need a colonoscopy, and you will? How they won't pay taxes? How they can fly without feathers; can, by will, as it were, lift themselves into the air?

Is it easier in life to admit you are alone or should one seek to make a camouflage of that fact? If you got one today, what might you name a dog? Have you ever been bitten by a blue jay? Do breasts not attract you as much as they once did? Would you make regular visits to a slaughterhouse if you could? Do you regard fondly or not fondly the theater of homosexuality?

What would we prepare if told that Einstein was coming to dinner? Would we set the dishes more carefully in the light? Would we, I mean, adjust the lighting? Would we microwave for him? If we were told that Einstein secretly carries a very small pet in his pocket, would we seek to discover what it is? Do you feel all right? Would you be embarrassed or rather thrilled by yourself if you were caught by Einstein with your hand in his coat pocket? Would you prefer to explain yourself in such a moment to Einstein, to Freud, or to Picasso? Are you not past the point of explaining yourself in earnest? Would you like to go to the big new grocery store and marvel at packaging? How have we gotten so stoned, on nothing? Can what we have come to be explained merely by fatigue? Are we possibly now not too far gone to wreak even the meager vengeance of snapping Juicy Fruit at the world?

Will our lips properly moisten for insouciance? Will our lips do what we want them to? Have our lips ever done what we wanted them to? Do you subscribe to the tumble-down theory of economics? What is the ratio of canaries to parakeets? Do you think that an animal that appears to mourn its dead, such as elephants, is capable of imagining its own death? Does fighting to preserve oneself intimate an imagining of one's death?

Are you leaving now? Would you? Would you mind?

About the author

About the book

Read on

Insights,
Interviews
& More . . .

Meet Padgett Powell

PADGETT POWELL is the author of four novels, including *Edisto*, which was nominated for the National Book Award, and two collections of stories. His writing has appeared in the *New Yorker*, *Harper's*, the *Paris Review*, *Esquire*, and other publications, as well as in the anthologies *Best American Short Stories* and *Best American Sports Writing*. He has received a Whiting Writers' Award and the Rome Fellowship in Literature from the American Academy of Arts and Letters. He lives in Gainesville, Florida, where he teaches writing at MFA@FLA, the writing program of the University of Florida. ⟋⟍

What Writing Should Do

For more than twenty years Padgett Powell has taught fiction writing at the University of Florida to both undergraduates and graduate students in the MFA program. As part of his course syllabus he often includes these guidelines:

KEEP IN MIND what writing should do:

1. Be alive
2. Be surprising
3. Obey tenets of economy, verve, etc.
4. Amount to something (usually, in terms of having "something at stake")
5. Pay off (i.e., resolve).

Any three of the five is worth spoiling paper for. It should be remembered also that:

6. Brave wild failure is applauded

And that:

7. You should be less comfortable if you're pretty sure of what you're writing about

And that:

8. You should ignore, at all times, all sense of authorial narrative obligations, and, certainly, your own preconceptions and ideas.

This is more preaching than could possibly be salubrious. So, some more: Obey only the logic of immediacy, from word to word. *Or*, obey only its obverse, the illogic of immediacy, or the logic of inimmediacy, as you prefer. ∿

A Short History of an Improbable Book

LET US SAY that one might have a colleague who invariably deploys the interrogative mood in instructing one on how to conduct his business at the university in which one works. Say one is the director of a program there. An e-mail might look like this: "Is it time for the director to have a chat with the provost? Do we recall what the dean promised us last spring? Would it be prudent to assume that history will not repeat itself?" And so forth.

Having received a number of such e-mails, I began to compose a rejoinder. "Should it not still be Constantinople? Do you love the velvet ant as much as I?" And so on. Imagining the fun of sending a chunk of this out Reply All, I got rolling, and I kept rolling for two hundred pages. I never sent a word of it to the intended. I did send it to a famous magazine, where an editor professed to love it, fashioned an excerpt, and then notified me on Christmas Eve while I languished in hundred-degree heat on the Muslim island of Lamu off the coast of Kenya that the magazine's editor "could not be convinced." Then I sent it to the *Paris Review*. An editor there bought a piece, and then, having left there for Ecco, bought the whole book.

I once thought that only young writers delivered themselves of books predicated on demonstrably insupportable ideas. Either I am wrong or in losing my mind I have become young again. ᴄᴗ

—Padgett Powell

Dude, C'est Moi

An Interview with Padgett Powell about *The Interrogative Mood*

The Faster Times: I have a question about the first question mark in *The Interrogative Mood: A Novel?*, which is right there in the subtitle. Is it really meant to question whether the book is a novel, or is it more of an insistence that this book composed entirely of questions is in fact a novel, or is it something else entirely?

Padgett Powell: That question mark is meant to diffuse the kind of irk that results, legitimately, when something that is arguably not a novel is called a novel. I was thinking specifically of Norman Mailer's *Why Are We in Vietnam*? It chapped some ass when it was called a novel. I sought not to chap but to still classify the odd document as a novel. What with all the question marks to follow, it seemed like a natural move to let one leak onto the title page.

The Faster Times: It makes me think, too, of David Markson's late quartet of novels, one of which is titled *This Is Not a Novel*. But now I'm curious: Did you set out to write a novel composed only of questions or did it begin as something else? Also, how did you decide to classify *The Interrogative Mood* as a novel and did you ever consider classifying it as something else? ▶

Dude, C'est Moi *(continued)*

Powell: It started and remained an answer to certain e-mails I was getting entirely in the interrogative mood. At no time did I plan a book, at no time did I submit it as a book to a book publisher. Calling a thing a novel helps it have a slim chance of someone's buying it.

The Faster Times: If you weren't planning on *The Interrogative Mood* being a book and it was never submitted as book, then how did all of those questions accumulate and how did it become a book?

Powell: I kept writing them, having nothing better to do after putting on my pants, depressed. I sent them to the *Paris Review*. An editor at the *Paris Review* bought some, quit *Paris Review*, took a job at Ecco, and called me from there saying they wanted to do the book. I said OK.

The Faster Times: That is one of the best publication stories that I have ever heard. Also, there was something about the tone of *The Interrogative Mood* that I hadn't quite figured out, something that I was fascinated with, something that allowed the narrator to ask questions about a huge range of subjects and also allowed all kinds of non sequiturs that I accepted without question—"depressed" makes that all make sense. Forgive the windup and here's the question: Are you, Padgett Powell, also the narrator of *The Interrogative Mood*, or is the narrator a fictional creation separate from you (or is the narrator maybe a fictional Padgett Powell)?

Powell: Dude, c'est moi. It's always c'est moi. Narrator schmarrator, author schmauthor.

The Faster Times: OK, let's go back to something else, the idea of originality. *The Interrogative Mood* is original, singular. That is what piqued my interest and that is why I kept reading. In fact, as I read deep into the novel, I began to see a double narrative at work. There was one novel, the narrator's novel, which the reader begins to discern to some extent through the adjectival nature of the questions, the fact that the questions have been chosen to be the particular questions in *The Interrogative Mood*. The second novel is the reader's novel, which the reader begins to create by answering the questions. I know there isn't a question there, but I thought you might want to say something about that.

Powell: I like "the adjectival nature of the questions," but confess I do not know what that means.

There is always, I suppose, a second novel, that of the reader, who is imagining things privately and differently from the way the writer imagined them; in this case, though, we do have the specific theater of the answers themselves, which the writer has not imagined for the reader, per se. That is not perhaps the exact correct usage of "per se," but don't it look smart?

***The Faster Times*:** That seems like a good place to end—with you asking a question. ∽

—Interview by Michael Kimball

This interview originally appeared on the Faster Times *website on January 27, 2010. Special thanks to Michael Kimball and the* Faster Times *for permission to reprint it.*

Selections from the Mailbag
Letters to Padgett Powell about *The Interrogative Mood*

Dear Professor Powell,

I am drunk. And you are not my professor. And, though I feel like a bashful Dickinson asking a suitor whether her verse is "alive," I wanted to ask before sobering up that you please read my review—in your spare time. It's more of an essay, or a trial, of *The Interrogative Mood: A Novel?* I wrote it for a two-man choir: my best friend, and you.

Yours, red-handedly,
J.C.

P.S. Thank you. Not for reading the article (because, frankly, whatever about that), but for the book I couldn't have put down if I tried. Really, thank you.

Ms. C:

I was drunk myself once, and arguably still am. I'll not be your professor. I am a webfudd so have to print your review to read it and could not find a print-friendly tab so just sent it to [the] printer, and we will see what I get. It opens looking like it is serious and among the best I have seen. On Amazon you can see another, by a twelve-year-old boy, though he does not boast of his age.

P Powell

Dear Mr. Powell,

    I found that I couldn't fully enjoy *The Interrogative Mood: A Novel?* unless I actually took the time to think about and answer each and every question. A few pages in I began feeling lost. To combat this I started writing down my answers hoping to find some sort of continuity, an "aha!" moment; anything.

    Next thing I know, I had answered every question in the book, and quite a few that came from my own head. I just want to thank you so much for sharing such a cool idea. I have included my answers in their entirety should you be interested in checking them out.

Thanks again,
J.

J.—

    I thank you. When I get to a printer and get some time, I will check out these answers. To have done them all strikes me as prodigious work. I could see a set of tight answers constituting a book on its own.

Padgett Powell

Dear Professor Powell:

    I am a musician currently pursuing a master's in music composition, and recently read *The Interrogative Mood* after hearing your segment on NPR. I was moved and transfixed by the piece and immediately recognized that portions of the text were exactly what I had been looking for as a "partial libretto" for my next mixed media chamber piece. In the interest of brevity, I won't bore you ▶

with details, but essentially I would like to juxtapose percussion, electronics, vocalizations, and a brief narrative about a couple living in a dystopian, imaginary future, with a series of questions borrowed from various sections of *The Interrogative Mood*. The questions would be spoken by a male and female standing at opposite ends of the concert hall, and small, processed chunks of these questions would also be part of the accompanying/surrounding electroacoustic soundscape.

This piece would be used for my master's recital, and will not produce any income for me. May I have your permission to use portions of *The Interrogative Mood* in this work?

I also assure you all proper attributions would be made in the program notes, and I can send you a recording of the work after the performance. Thank you for your consideration.

Best regards,
D.D.

Mr. D—
I see no harm. Proceed with your evil plan. I shall copy two adults so they know what we are up to and can stop you or deflect you if need be. We'll later develop your libretto for the stage play.

P Powell

Padgett Powell,
Does everyone write to you now with only questions? Is it tiresome? Are you the first person on earth to write a novel in the interrogative mode? Will you go down in literary history? When was your birthday? Once you've begun questioning, is it possible to stop? I can't stop—do I have OCD? Should I delete this and start over? Are you going to delete this e-mail this minute? If I don't write anything interesting soon will you delete? I didn't answer one question in your novel—did you think people would? If the landscape of a book reminds you how much you long for things that have left you, how much regret you hope to be redeemed by, of the humor you use for comfort—and in that book the author lets you glimpse the bit of bravery you must have and will have, you hope—then will

you actually write him and thank him or do you just think you should? Will I delete this e-mail?

Thanks for *The Interrogative Mood*.

A.B.

A.B.—

Good letter, girl. I will answer two: I did not think people would or should answer and am a little made nervous by those (many) who report that they did. And "if the landscape . . .": The compliment in this question is one of the best I have received, and I thank YOU for it. It should be on [the] flap.

Padgett Powell

Dear Dr. Powell,

A group of about twenty-five Unitarian Universalist Fellowship members gathers every other month for a couple of hours to discuss a book we have recently read. The group has accepted my recommendation that we read and discuss *The Interrogative Mood*? at its [next] meeting. We meet from 4 to 6 P.M. We range in age from the 50s into the 90s, and not a few of us are retired faculty from several institutions. Conversation is accompanied by appetizers and a range of beverages (mostly wine).

We would be delighted to have you join us for that discussion. Will you? Why not!? What if we agree to address you only with questions? We may even accept your being in the mood to do the same with us. Or not.

Cordially, B.A.

Mr. A—

I am happy to entertain an evening with your group. . . . I'd prefer to be addressed by no questions, if we engage. I have no answers and do not purport to illuminate anything.

P Powell

Professor Powell,

Congratulations, your terrific book *The Interrogative Mood* will be an instant classic. But in response to the "?," it might not be a novel. ▶

Selections from the Mailbag *(continued)*

It seems to me that it shows rather than tells issues raised by the philosophy/way of life of Pyrrhonism, in which the problem of the criterion leads to suspension of judgment and skepsis—always searching—which would make it a one-of-a-kind document in philosophy. Whatever it is? Thanks for writing it.

P.W.

[No response.] ❧

Author's Picks
An Abecedarium

I WANT TO PROMOTE my own students—
a fair thing to do—and to be fair within
fair will commence at the beginning:
ABCD.

A

Chris Adrian

He went on to become a doctor and
has yet to send me the narcotics he said
he would. Cf. his story collection, *A Better
Angel* (Farrar, Straus and Giroux, 2008).

B

Chris Bachelder

The wickedest, funniest good writer in
the country. This is the calm, measured
assessment of a daddy. Cf. *Bear v. Shark*
(Scribner, 2001) and *U.S.!* (Bloomsbury
USA, 2006).

C

Kevin Canty and Kevin Wilson

Canty, because his "Pretty Judy" is
the one in thirty years of student stories
I wish I'd written or stolen. Cf. his latest
story collection, *Where the Money Went*
(Nan A. Talese, 2009). And Wilson,
because you must list pairs when they
become available, as PBS must show
photos of the fallen when they become
available, and because when I suggested
he use his infant as a trolling motor he
wrote "The Nuclear-Battery Baby." Cf.
his story collection, *Tunneling to the
Center of the Earth* (Ecco, 2009). ▶

Author's Picks *(continued)*

D

Pete Dexter

Not a student of mine but someone of whom I am, somewhat less than I should be, a student. Mr. Dexter does that old Hemingway Zen thing of trying to say exactly what you feel in lieu of what you ought to feel or have been taught to feel, and if you get it right, it is true for ten years or forever, to roughly paraphrase Papa Boor himself. Read the new, odd book *Spooner* (Grand Central, 2009), the old classic *Paris Trout* (Random House, 1988), and, even better, the sneaky, frightening *The Paperboy* (Random House, 1995). Pete and I go back to 1983, when a review in *Time* magazine launched my book *Edisto* ahead of his first book, *God's Pocket*, and I flashed to stardom and Pete sank. By our third books, I was broke and walking plank at my publisher, and Pete had won the National Book Award. Top man on bottom, bottom man on top rail. Roughhousing with a puppy he was recently nipped and nearly died of a staph infection and is not out of the woods yet, so we should all pull for Pete. ❧

—Padgett Powell

Don't miss the next book by your favorite author. Sign up now for AuthorTracker by visiting www.AuthorTracker.com.

37690100R00117

Made in the USA
Lexington, KY
10 December 2014